MAUI HOLIDAZE

A CHRISTMAS HOLIDAY STORY

PARADISE CRIME COZY MYSTERIES
BOOK 4

TOBY NEAL

To all the people and pets everywhere, who wake up at the holidays with magic in their eyes. ~Toby Neal

"Dear George: Remember no man is a failure who has friends."
~It's a Wonderful Life (1946)

1

MY CAT TIKI WAS DEMANDING, prone to violence, loud, and loving. She made her feelings about me abundantly clear: wherever I was, that's where she wanted to be—and to heck with the inconvenience to me or anyone else.

That's why, when I woke up alone in my big bed, stretching my very tall body to its limits so that my fingers and toes reached over both edges of the king-size mattress, I was surprised not to bonk into my big fat cat. Tiki was usually right beside me, on top of my legs, or attempting to drape herself over my head like a hot furry hat.

Which, since we lived in the warm tropics on the island of Maui, was not pleasant.

Also, because—fleas. *shudder*

Or the possibility of them, which I kept at bay by feeding Tiki those pills that made her fur toxic and luring her into a monthly bath.

If I could have trained Tiki to sleep somewhere else, I would've, but Tiki was a former feral cat, and just getting her to comply with basic human/feline interspecies politeness was a big ask.

I'd also have loved for her to sleep somewhere else because she was a romance killer with my boyfriend Keone when he tried to visit. Tiki didn't like us being together in what she considered HER bed; she was as possessive and jealous as that rather terrifying Hawaiian goddess, Pele.

I sat up and tossed my covers off, straightening my sleep tee, a mid-thigh number that featured Jessica Rabbit striking a come-hither pose. Aunt Fae had given it to me to assist with my relationship, which was endearing given she was a lifelong singleton herself. Auntie was all atwitter that I had a boyfriend, let alone one of Keone's hot pilot caliber. She thought Jessica Rabbit sent the right message.

I could hardly blame Auntie for being surprised by the ongoing presence of "Mr. K" as I fondly called him. I'd never had a relationship for this long. Ever.

Yep, I had issues. Somewhat like those of my cat, as a matter of fact.

"Tiki?" I padded across the floor of my enormous bedroom and climbed onto the bench seat that looked out behind the house. I peered out the wide bay window, scanning the grounds for my favorite one-eared, kink-tailed calico feline. If Tiki saw something huntable outside, she'd stalk off to catch it, but since we'd moved into these cushy digs where she was provided on-demand meals, she was getting lazy. She hadn't brought in a rat, bird, or lizard for months.

Alas, my reformed hellcat wasn't outside in the yard; nothing to see but mowed grass, swaying palms, and hibiscus bushes.

My gaze followed the empty street that wound past the cul-de-sac (of which we were the only house) to the hill at the top of the onetime subdivision. A Greek Revival mansion had been mapped out there by the gangster who'd planned this neighborhood, but the whole development had reverted to the state of Hawaii recently. New Ohia State Park was now owned by the public, and the Chang build site was to be turned into a children's soccer field.

I smiled with satisfaction; I'd had a little something to do with all of that.

I turned away from the pretty view and got dressed. I had an important job as the postmaster of the tiny town of Ohia, and as my friend and coworker Pua Chang always said, "The mail must go on."

My Aunt Fae was already downstairs, toasting a couple of slices of famous Hana banana bread in the countertop toaster oven of our former model home.

"That smells criminally good," I said, tucking the tail of a white polo shirt into my work pants. "Got enough for me, too?"

"Of course I have enough for you." Aunt Fae took an old-fashioned butter dish off the counter and opened the lid.

She'd had a friend packing up and sending favorite things that she'd left at her house in Maine, now that she'd relocated to live with me. This piece was one I remembered well: heavy old China in the shape of a little red hen sitting on a nest. You picked up the hen by a knob on her back in the shape of a round yellow chick. Butter rested inside, soft at room temperature and ready to soak into a sweet-smelling slice of slightly crisp, but moist, banana bread.

Yes, I liked food. At six foot one with an active metabolism, I could slather high calorie substances on whatever I wanted and zip my jeans without sucking in my stomach. I didn't take that for granted; I worked at keeping in shape. That level of athleticism used to be part of my career as a Secret Service agent; now it was just a part of my life.

I poured a cup of Kona coffee and slid onto a stool at the breakfast bar to watch Auntie spackle calories onto the banana bread. She handed me a yogurt and a spoon as well. "You need some protein with your sweets."

I rolled my eyes but didn't argue; she was right. I dug into the yogurt first, watching the butter melting into the tasty banana bread toast. "Have you seen Tiki this morning?"

"Nope." Auntie pointed to Tiki's dish on the floor near the pantry. "But she's had breakfast already."

"Probably out hunting something." I finished the yogurt and bit into the banana bread. "Oh. My. Yum."

"Mmm," Auntie agreed through a mouthful of her own delicious treat. Silence reigned as we savored, smiling at each other.

I'd been used to my career-woman Secret Service solo existence but Aunt Fae, my beloved guardian, joining me as a roomie was the culmination of a longing to live with family that I hadn't dared put into words.

My phone chirped, making me jump. I was still getting used to the device working. New Ohia Park, where we lived, had a satellite Wi-Fi hookup that worked better than anything else in town. A glance at the screen showed that the call was from Security Solutions, an international firm where I was occasionally employed as an investigator. "Good morning. This is Kat."

"Hullo to my favorite Secret Service agent." My boss Sophie Smithson's plummy Brit tones were upbeat this morning. Sometimes she sounded like a mile of bad road; she had two toddlers at home. Rumor had it that was like SEAL training with additional sleep deprivation torture.

"No longer with the Service, Sophie. My resignation papers went through last week." I chased a blot of melted butter around my plate with a fingertip as a twinge of pain tightened my chest.

Was I sad that I'd left my former career? Once in a while, yeah —which usually meant I needed to go for a swim with the turtles or a surf with Mr. K to remind myself why I'd chosen a life in Ohia.

"Oh, right. Sorry." Sophie cleared her throat. "Do you have a moment? I have a lead on a job for you."

"Sure. Christmas is coming. I could use some extra cash." I caught Auntie's eye, and she gave a thumbs up. The model home we lived in needed personalization, for sure. We'd moved into the place furnished in generic "beach chic," which was fine—but the house lacked the personality that items like Aunt Fae's butter dish conveyed.

Plus we'd always loved doing the holidays big. Between Auntie's pension and my postmaster salary, there wasn't much extra left over to buy gifts, decorations, and baking supplies, let alone specialty items like a partridge in a pear tree or an elf for the shelf.

"I'm pleased to hear that. This job is actually too small for Security Solutions to take on, but I told the woman who called us you might be able to help." I heard the rattle of Sophie's keyboard in the background as she spoke; she was a computer whiz and always multitasking. "Puny French fries, as they say, but urgent to the client. A woman in Hana is missing her beloved cat. She called us to help find it when her efforts failed to turn the feline up."

"Puny French fries? You mean, 'small potatoes.'" English was a second language to Sophie and that occasionally showed up in her usage of slang. "Hmm. A missing cat?" I glanced instinctively at Tiki's empty food bowl. "I don't need to know more than that. I'll take the job."

2

THE POST OFFICE was busy this Friday morning in the first week of December; that was true everywhere in the United States, I'm sure, but we were a remote, rural outpost. The onslaught of online ordering had hit us hard. We were too small to have mail delivery, so we had to sort deliveries into the postboxes.

Now, that should have been easy. We only had a hundred of those. But for every package that arrived, we marked a slip and put it into the box, then handed out the package personally when the customer arrived and presented their slip to us for pickup. In addition, the hundred postal boxes were inadequate by far for the five hundred-ish residents living in the village of Ohia. That meant those slips had to be filled out and stashed in General Delivery slots as well.

Needless to say, my partner Pua Chang and I barely had time to take a pee during business hours in December. And every day, Chad the delivery dude pulled up in his USPS truck and off-loaded bags, bundles, boxes, and entire pallets of goods like a skinny, pimply North Pole worker with a bad attitude.

I was the bigger and stronger of the two of us staffers, so I helped Chad with the towering piles of boxes and bags. "You know, most of these packages are probably gifts. We're the real Santas. How does that make you feel?" I huffed, lifting a heap of boxes out of the rear of the truck, and using my knees as recommended.

"Bah, humbug," Chad snorted.

"Maybe this will help." Setting down the boxes, I handed Chad a paper plate I'd brought out for him, loaded with chocolate chip macadamia nut cookies and Kona coffee fudge that Aunt Fae had made. She'd been up at all hours baking for the holidays and trying out new recipes now that she'd joined me in Hawaii all the way from Maine.

"*Mele Kalikimaka*, as they say here. I recommend a hit of the coffee fudge for your drive back to Kahului. It has more kick than an espresso."

Chad's gloomy expression brightened. The kid ripped into the red transparent plastic covering the treats, grabbed a chunk of fudge, and crammed it into his mouth. He shut his eyes and chewed for a long minute; he really did look tired.

"Good," he grunted, and stowed the plate on the passenger seat. "Let's get this done."

"That's what I'm here for," I said with determined cheerfulness. I've always believed in trying to set an example, and though I was as overwhelmed as Chad by the sheer amount of mail, letting that show wasn't good for morale. We hefted the final stack of boxes and wheeled them inside on the dolly, off-loading them beside the big steel table where Pua had already dumped out all the letter mail for sorting.

Pua waved to Chad with her purple latex gloves. "Thank you for all the hard work."

Darned if he didn't smile and say, "Happy holidays, ladies. You make the drive out here worthwhile."

And what a drive it was! Located on the "backside" of the island, the road to Hana that led through Ohia was rough, narrow, and winding. The route was also beautiful and scenic, but when you had a job to do and a schedule to keep, that was harder to appreciate.

As Chad pulled away in the truck, I slanted a glance at Pua. "I'm thinking we need to keep that boy supplied with goodies through the holidays."

"Yes, and we have the perfect ongoing supply." My colleague held up a plastic platter of peanut butter balls dipped in chocolate. "The customers keep dropping off treats. Let's pass them along to Chad."

My stomach rumbled at the sight. "With a pause for tax to me." I pried up a corner of the cellophane wrap covering the balls and popped one in my mouth. "Mmm. We call these buckeyes on the continent."

Pua patted her slim hip. "I'll take your word for it. I'll have to take Sassy for an extra mile walk if I eat one of those." Sassy was Pua's yappy little dog and yes, that pooch definitely needed a calming walk daily.

"I'm more of a cat person, as you know. Speaking of, I've heard of a cat gone missing in Hana." I produced the color print flyer I'd made of the missing Himalayan that Sophie had asked me to locate. "I'm taking a little side job looking for this beauty."

Pua admired the cat, who was posed sitting regally on an ice-blue satin pillow that matched her eyes. Well-groomed, flowing fur draped around her like a queen's robes. "Wow. Looks like an indoor cat. Wonder how she escaped?"

"I have no idea yet how she disappeared. I have to contact the owner, but I thought I'd start the hunt by talking to our customers. Not much gets by the 'coconut wireless' around here." I lifted the old-fashioned counter flap and headed over to the bulletin board with the flyer. I'd added my number to the bottom on a series of tear-off strips, and I pinned it up prominently. "I'll be posting these around town and asking people if they've seen Lady Sapphire."

"Is this one of your investigative side jobs?" Pua asked as she restocked supplies for the counter.

"Yes. My first one, actually. The job was too small for Security Solutions on Oahu to take, but Sophie punted me the lead. K & K Investigations will be taking on the recovery of this beautiful kitty as our first official job." Between the time I'd got the call from Sophie and the start of the day at the post office, I'd found a few minutes to call my partner and boyfriend Keone Kaihale and forward him a copy of the cat flyer. Keone would be posting and sharing it around the Hana Airport as he made his flight run of the day to Kahului.

"I hope you find her soon," Pua said, a wrinkle between her perfectly groomed brows. "She looks valuable."

I shrugged. "Every pet is valuable to its owner." Even Tiki, the stray I'd had no choice in adopting because she chose me first. Tiki's crooked tail and one-eared profile had become as dear to me as any purebred animal could be. "I'm going to make a quick call to the owner before we open the post office doors."

I hurried to my admin work area and shut the door. Scrolling on my phone to the number Sophie had given me for the missing cat's owner, I called it. "Mrs. Scarborough? This is Kat Smith with K & K Investigations."

"Oh yes." An elderly woman's voice replied, reedy and thin. "Ms. Smithson with Security Solutions told me to expect your call. Thanks for being so prompt. I am just beside myself about Lady's disappearance."

"I have her photo already made into a flyer, and we're circulating it beginning today. Tell me more about how she ran away."

"Oh, she didn't run away. Someone took her from my garden. It's fenced so she can't get out. I would never let her roam, nor would she want to." Mrs. Scarborough's voice broke on the last sentence, and she sniffled. "She's my faithful companion."

I told her I'd send an hourly contract with a bonus for positive completion to her by email, then got more details.

Lady Sapphire had a cat door that led from the kitchen into the walled garden area where the cat "liked to sit in the sun and maybe watch a butterfly or two float by." She had disappeared from the garden, whose gate was kept closed but not locked, a week ago. Mrs. Scarborough had been combing her neighborhood in Hana and posting on social media ever since.

My heart sank a little; a week was a long time for a cat that valuable to be missing. Someone had probably stolen her, especially when Mrs. Scarborough disclosed that the cat had recently been bred to a champion sire and was expecting kittens. "Each one of them will be worth thousands, but that's not what I care about so much as her going through the birth alone. Her first litter! She will be terrified without me."

Cats, in my experience, were confident and self-sufficient animals who chose to tolerate and like humans for their own reasons. Tiki had been occupying the shack that went with the postmaster job I'd been assigned to when I arrived in Ohia. Over the course of a few months, we'd bonded—but I still never knew what to expect from her.

As today's apparent desertion had shown me.

But perhaps Lady Sapphire, a purebred domesticated cat, had a more symbiotic relationship with her owner.

"I hope I'll be able to find her for you quickly. When are the kittens due?"

"The week of Christmas. I am a woman alone; my family is all gone. I thought the arrival of kittens would liven up the holiday for both of us." Mrs. Scarborough was referring to the cat as a life companion. She sniffled again. "Let me know the moment you know anything."

"I will, of course. I'd like to come by this afternoon and hear more about her daily habits and see where she was snatched," I said.

We agreed on a time, and I hung up the phone with a sinking feeling. Finding a valuable cat that had been stolen was a lot different than one that had just wandered off.

3

I POINTED to the photo of Lady Sapphire taped to the counter as I handed over a General Delivery package to my umpteenth customer of the day. "This cat is missing. Have you seen her?"

"Oh no! That's Elvira Scarborough's cat, Lady. She must be so upset!" Mrs. Fukagawa, an octogenarian and honorary member of the Red Hat Society, wore her scarlet sun hat today. She adjusted the reading specs dangling from a beaded chain that she'd slid on to inspect both the photo and her package. "What happened to her?"

"Mrs. Scarborough thinks she was stolen. She disappeared from the fenced garden," I said.

"Well, that's strange. Lady's the fourth missing cat I've heard about lately."

My stomach already had a knot in it. Though Mrs. Fukagawa was the first to know Mrs. Scarborough and her cat personally, she wasn't the first to tell me about the rash of missing felines in our area.

My mind flew once more to Tiki. I'd sneaked in a text to Aunt Fae to see if my missing pet had shown back up at home. She had not. "Were the cats you heard about stolen, or did they run away?"

"A bit of both." Mrs. Fukagawa drew her package closer. "Is there anything else for me?"

A line was forming behind Mrs. Fukagawa; customers were eager to get their packages. I pretended she was asking if she could help with the investigation and not about more mail. "As a matter of fact, there is." I grabbed a pen and lined tablet and thrust them at Mrs. Fukagawa. "Anything you can remember about the missing pets might help us find Lady. Maybe there's a reason why so many cats are gone at once." I sweetened the request by grabbing one of the buckeyes in its little ruffled cup off the platter and plunking it down on top of the lined tablet. "A little thank-you gift for your help."

Mrs. Fukagawa grinned. She was missing a side molar but somehow it made her smile, bracketed in soft velvety wrinkles, even more charming. "Why, thank you. I'll step aside and work on that."

She took the tablet and the treat, and my next customer stepped into her place. I pointed to Lady's photo after I fetched the woman's mail. "Have you seen this missing cat?"

And thus it went for several more customers.

Eventually Mrs. Fukagawa elbowed her way up to the front of the line. She slid the tablet, now covered in crabbed writing, over to me. "Another of those tasty peanut butter goodies, please."

"Happy to oblige." I passed her the buckeye. "I hope you put your number on there in case I need to follow up with anything."

"I sure did." She tapped the pad. "Let me know how it goes."

By lunchtime I was frazzled and, judging by the slight shine on Pua's perfect little nose, so was she—but I took my break first. I planned to check in with Mr. K and review Mrs. Fukagawa's notes. "See you at one p.m.," I told her. "I'll be out in the shack."

Pua nodded, already engaged with the next customer—and as I glanced into the sorting area, I was pleased to see the mountain of packages was shrinking.

The shack behind the post office was assigned housing for the postmaster. That was my main job, so the space was still available to me to use. After Aunt Fae and I moved to the unoccupied model home in New Ohia, I had checked with my boss Mr. Hanoi in Kahului if it would be okay to use it as an office from which to operate our side business instead of living in the humble quarters. He was agreeable.

I glanced around the perimeter of the shack with affection.

Keone and I had transplanted the coconut palm that had taken root in the gutter to a more appropriate spot beside the building, and the baby tree had already thrown out a new frond in gratitude. The ginger on one side was healthy and the hibiscus bush beside the little porch was blooming, its red blossoms bright against the green foliage.

"A new kind of Christmas red and green," I murmured, snapping a picture with my phone. I was collecting Maui images to send to my friends and former Secret Service colleagues in a holiday e-card along with a general update about my status as a full-time resident of Ohia.

I'd put a lot into my career with the Secret Service; never anticipating the turn my life would take when I ended up on temporary assignment as postmaster in Ohia after a handsy Congressman I'd rejected had disrupted my plans with his vendetta.

So far, I didn't regret the difficult decision to trade the drafty halls of politics in Washington, DC for a simpler life across the street from a beach on Maui.

I grabbed the broom leaning in a corner of the porch and gave the simple structure a brisk sweep, including the large coral stone beach rock that made up the front step.

I couldn't sweep it without remembering the initial "gift" Tiki had brought me the first day I moved in—the withered hand of the woman who'd had the postmaster job before me. That investigation had led to the next, and the next—and now I happily used the broom to whisk any dust and cobwebs off the simple plaque Mr. K had attached to the door that read *K & K Investigations.*

Done with my domestic duties, I unlocked the entry and flipped on the light. We'd made some improvements to the space: Mr. K had rewired the dangling string lights to actual switches, and we'd worked together to cut a small window in the wall facing the front porch, so now a breeze from the direction of Ohia Bay could blow through the shack and out the window that faced into the jungle at the rear. I opened the window, sliding the glass aside but keeping the screen in place, and also unlatched and propped open the back window; the place smelled a little musty, which happened quickly here in the tropics.

I glanced at the kitchenette area that lined one wall. The interior appeared bug-free, and over our months sharing the space I'd come to have a fondness for the critters that called it home.

"Hello, Tweedledum. Tweedledee." The two geckos stuck to the wall, one with a stumpy tail from Tiki's attempt to eat it, pumped their bodies up and down in greeting. "And Miss Prissy." I was less fond of the large brown cane spider perched in the corner but had accepted her bug-catching prowess along with that of the geckos as part of island living. "I see you guys got those flies that came in when I opened the door last time. Thanks."

I grabbed a dishtowel and wiped down the old Formica table. Keone and I had added office chairs on either side of it and put in a satellite-enabled router that hooked into New Ohia's system; that white device sat on the table like a squat Internet deity, waiting to connect me to the outside world.

I had also brought my lunch, a glass storage container of Aunt Fae's delicious corn chowder with a side of homemade bread. I threw the chowder in the microwave and sat down in my office chair, taking out my phone. I tried video call and was rewarded by the sight of Keone's very white smile. "Hey, Mr. K. Can you talk?"

"Sure, Kitty Kat. I'm at Kahului Airport between flights." I'd hoped that would be the case; in response to his moniker (he'd taken to calling me what my dear friend Artie from the Ohia General Store had dubbed me), I loved the way the nickname rolled off his tongue with a Polynesian lilt. "How's the Lady Sapphire hunt going at your end?"

I dug the piece of lined paper out of my pocket and squinted at Mrs. Fukagawa's chicken scratch. "Pretty concerning, actually. I verified that Lady Sapphire was stolen, in her owner's opinion, due to being in a closed garden she couldn't get out of when she disappeared. She's also been gone a week with no sightings, which isn't great. And she was preggers and due to have valuable pedigreed kittens at Christmas."

"Maybe she was stolen so her babies could be sold. The plot thickens. "

"Yes, it does. Especially since there have been a bunch of missing loose cats in our area. Several customers verified it. I got one of the customers to write down all she knew, but her handwriting is hard to read."

I set the phone in a prop-up holder so we could see each other, and I smoothed the paper out on the table, squinting at it. "Mrs. Fukagawa knows of five missing cats from the Hana and Ohia area. They were all indoor-outdoor felines. She says here some might have been taken from yards and some were loose and never came home."

My gaze fell to the folded beach towel under the table where Tiki hung out when I was here. I couldn't bear to tell Keone that Tiki might be missing too. She'd probably turn up by dinnertime, so it wasn't worth mentioning. "What did you find out at your end?"

He cleared his throat. "Are you sitting down?"

Well, dang. This did not bode well. "Keone, that sounds ominous."

I glanced over at the Murphy bed I'd slept on for my first months on Maui. Strapped securely to the wall, it promised a nap if I ever needed one. My three critter "pets" were happily hunting bugs on the wall in the kitchen, and through the back window I watched the large, glossy, waving leaves of a noni tree whose many health benefits my Hawaiian friend Josie had taught me about. Whatever news Keone had, I could handle it. "Tell me."

"Well, cats are disappearing here in Kahului too. Once I started showing the flyer and asking around, I heard about feral cats near the airport just up and disappearing. About twenty cats total so far. Most of a colony."

That gave me a bit of a chill. "You have feral cat colonies in that part of the island?"

"Yeah. You're new here so maybe you're not aware, but Maui has a feral cat overpopulation problem. They have no natural predators in Hawaii, and getting cats fixed is too expensive for a lot of people. Over time we've ended up with thousands on all the islands, but Maui especially."

"Yikes," I said.

"And the native bird and monk seal biologists—you know we have bird species and a seal species not found anywhere else in the world—they say the cats prey on the endangered birds and carry toxoplasmosis that kills the female monk seals. They are not fans. That pits them against the Cat People."

"Cat people?" I stared thoughtfully at Tiki's empty towel bed. "I'm a cat person, I guess. Because I love my cat."

"That's not the same. There are . . . *Cat People.*" His voice lowered to a hushed, spooky tone, making me smile. "My mom's one of them. These folks are passionate. They hate to see any cat put down for any reason. Cat People feed the wild cat colonies and pay for them to be spayed, neutered, and have vet care. One of the women who works with me in the baggage department is a Cat Person. She's part of caring for the airport cat colony, and she's the one that told me that the twenty or so from her group have disappeared."

Alertness rippled down my spine and I sat up straighter. "Who, or what, could remove that many cats all at once? And where would they go?"

"Nobody knows. Folks are upset and think they must have come to harm."

"Maybe they were trapped and taken somewhere to be rehomed," I said.

"On Maui?" He snorted. "We're an island, and a small one at that. The very definition of a feral cat is that it's wild and hard to find a home for. These animals aren't socialized. Like Tiki was when you first moved into the shack with her. Not everyone has your patience to win over a shy furry beast."

"Tiki was never shy."

"But most of them are, and are afraid of people."

I'd discovered Tiki the first day I moved into the shack as post-master; she'd already been inside and had no intention of leaving. And Tiki had, indeed, been a difficult roommate who'd drawn blood on more than one occasion. I'd never been called patient before, but in Tiki's case I guess I'd made an exception because we'd eventually found our groove.

Now it hurt to imagine life without her, and I hoped I wouldn't have to.

The microwave dinged, and I jumped, startled. "Okay. Well, there's a lot going on here, but we don't know if any of it is connected to our actual case. I'm going out to visit the scene of the crime, Elvira Scarborough's house, after work at four p.m. When will you be off? Maybe we can meet up in Hana."

"Yeah, I'd love an evening surf." Keone rolled his big shoulders in the tight white polyester uniform Pacific Wings packed him into. I loved the way he looked in it—yeah, I objectified my man, and he assured me that was okay. "My last flight of the day lands at five so I should be out of Hana Airport by five thirty—but there won't be much time to get in the water before it's dark now that it's December. Let's plan to go in at Koki Beach and we can eat at a food truck after." He smiled. Dang it, the guy had a cute dimple. "Can't wait to see you."

"Yup. Sounds like a plan."

"Love you," he said.

"Back atcha," I replied, and hit a button to end the call.

Saying the L word was still hard; I was vulnerable every time I admitted my feelings and so I found ways to avoid articulating them. I hoped he didn't notice.

I still had time to eat my corn chowder and dunk the bread in it, and I stared thoughtfully into space as I did so.

Who was making cats disappear on Maui? And why? What was happening to them?

That last question made the hairs rise on the back of my neck.

4

I TEXTED Aunt Fae about my plans to go to Hana as I bid Pua goodbye for the day. We locked up the post office at our usual closing time of four p.m. at the end of after another whirlwind of mail distribution.

I needed some exercise to unkink myself from the hectic pace of preholiday postal fun, so I decided to take the e-bike I kept plugged in and charged inside the shack. Once inside the K & K office (aka the shack) again, I put my bathing suit on under my clothes for my planned trip to Koki Beach with Keone after I visited our new client.

Originally Keone's mom's transport, Ilima Kaihale had loaned her e-bike to me with the caveat that I wore a lurid yellow visibility vest and helmet with a flashing light on the top every time I took it out. With the Ugliest Vest and Helmet on, I was hard to miss even on the tortuously narrow jungle road between Ohia and the larger town of Hana, where Mrs. Scarborough lived.

I enjoyed the tropical-scented wind in my hair as the battery-assist bike whizzed along the narrow route with its overgrown shoulders. I dodged loose chickens, mynah birds, and the occasional fallen mango in the road. There were several scenic hairpin turns where I could feast my eyes on the ocean if the tourist drivers clogging the road weren't also doing so; when they were, we were all in danger.

I had the route memorized, though, so I soon made it to Hana and my phone's trusty GPS guided me to Mrs. Scarborough's house.

Viewing the older plantation style home tucked beneath a large old-growth monkeypod tree near the church in the middle of town, I discovered why my client thought her cat had to have been removed by a human: the yard was enclosed by a tall wooden fence topped by decorative, pointed finials.

No cat in the world could climb out of there on its own.

Lowering daylight cast shadows across the yard as I parked the e-bike out front. Mrs. Scarborough answered the door quickly, as if she'd been waiting anxiously behind it. Her white hair hung uncombed to her shoulders and her thin frame in a faded muumuu was hunched with worry. Dark circles underscored eyes reddened from tears.

"Have you found Lady?" she asked, her voice wobbly.

I shook my head. "Not yet, but I'm hoping my visit here will provide some new clues."

Her shoulders slumped in disappointment. She waved me inside listlessly. "Please, look around all you'd like. I just want my Lady home."

"May I see where Lady's cat door was installed?"

"Of course."

The interior of the house was tidy but dated. Photos of happier times dotted shelves and side tables, their subjects' smiles in stark contrast to Mrs. Scarborough's palpable despair.

The older woman led me through quiet halls and directed me to the back door of the kitchen, where a rectangular plastic flap had been cut into the lower panel of the door. I squatted and peered outside through the cat door. "Can I look around the garden?"

"Of course."

Just as Mrs. Scarborough had described, the garden was fully enclosed by the tall wooden fence I'd seen from the outside. A square of tufty grass in the center of the area was surrounded by weed-choked flowerbeds flush with the tall fence. "The gate is always kept closed," she said, pointing to a gate with a hasp. "And you can't open it from the outside unless you reach over the top and undo it."

"Maybe whoever took Lady entered through the house," I said.

Elvira Scarborough frowned. "I don't lock the front door. No one does in Hana. So I guess that's possible."

I examined the perimeter carefully but saw no fingerprints, scratches, or other evidence of tampering on the sturdy planks.

We spent close to an hour or so together as I asked her numerous questions. Had any repairs been done, had any unfamiliar people visited, was there anything out of the ordinary in her home in the past weeks?

Mrs. Scarborough shook her head each time, at a loss.

Finally, I gently steered our conversation to the upcoming holidays. "What were your plans before Lady disappeared?" Small talk seemed the kindest way to lift her spirits, if only temporarily.

She offered a wan smile. "We were going to trim the tree together and cuddle by the wood stove in the living room while we waited for her kittens to arrive. Now it doesn't feel much like Christmas at all." Her eyes grew damp once more as she gazed at Lady's favorite spot to sun on the back porch.

I thanked Mrs. Scarborough for her time and made my exit, feeling stumped. I could only hope Keone might turn up with something new over dinner to reinvigorate our investigation before the trail grew completely cold.

5

RIDING the bike down the road from Hana back to Ohia, the evening grew dark as tangled tropical trees blocked what little sunlight remained of the day. I hurried, pedaling while visibility held, turning left into pastureland where the last rays of the sun caressed the lush grass where cattle grazed peacefully. And I was thankful when Koki Beach emerged ahead on the left of the turnoff, golden sand glowing softly in the sunset, the nearby atoll known as 'Ālau Island topped by coconut palms and ironwoods, providing a shadowy backdrop.

Keone's board-laden truck was parked at the far end of the beach, where a dirt path led down to surf crashing in the deepening colors of the sunset. I pulled up beside the truck as he emerged from the cab and picked up a board. He tucked it under a muscular arm in anticipation of our evening session before full night fell.

"Kitty Kat," he called with a smile. "Rough today, eh?"

I nodded wearily, dismounting and pushing the bike over to join him. "No leads at the crime scene except that I confirmed that Lady Sapphire could not have escaped Mrs. Scarborough's yard on her own."

"Well, let's hit the waves. Recharge our brain cells and compare notes after. The moon's rising as the sun sets, and once our eyes adjust, it should be enough." He had already taken the longboard I'd been learning on off the racks and set it against the truck for me. "Here's your stick."

"Night surfing. This is a first." I stripped off the helmet, vest, and clothing I'd worn over my bathing suit, draping them over the bike's rear rack. "As if I wasn't already a terrible surfer."

"No substitute for water time," Keone said, handing me a rash guard. "That ought to help keep you warm."

I slid the tight, stretchy shirt on and rolled it down over my bikini. "And keep my suit in place."

He leaned in to give me a quick kiss. "No one around tonight but us. We could skinny-dip."

"Read my lips: heck, no."

Keone laughed and turned toward the beach. "Last one in is a rotten noni fruit!"

Since I knew what those smelled like (carrion, no joke), I grabbed the longboard and chased him into the chilly, rolling waves.

An hour or so of badly lit ocean water whomping followed with Keone showing off his moves, per usual, and me wiping out.

I finally caught one wave and was able to ride it all the way in, though, and decided to call that good.

I sat on the beach and watched my boyfriend "rip" as they called good surfing here in Hawaii. Boy was he fun to watch, even backlit by a rising moon. He loved to do fin-first reversals and other tricks including off-the-lip and "getting air."

I clapped as Mr. K walked up out of the gleaming white foam facing me, his broad grin a gleam of white teeth in the dim light. "That was great, Keone!"

"I saw that wave you caught," he said. "You might not think so, but you're getting better."

Keone and I wrapped in warm towels, and he led the way to a

lone food truck that had set up at the opposite end of the beach, ordering us each a healthy meal. Between bites of teriyaki steak stir-fry bowl at the picnic table in the beachfront hut, I recounted my fruitless visit to Mrs. Scarborough's home in detail. Maybe some new angle might emerge that Keone's keen pilot's eyes would see.

But his level brows only furrowed deeper, contemplating the mystery.

"Don't lose hope," he insisted when I'd finished my story. "I have an idea."

I perked up, snagging onto this thread. "Lay it on me, Mr. K!"

Keone smiled at my enthusiasm, shaking his head. "It's no big breakthrough, but when I stopped for gas, I ran into one of the bird biologists that monitors 'Ālau Island's bird population." He pointed to the outcrop of land off the point, crowned by a cluster of palm trees. "When I asked about missing cats, the scientist said he was glad there were fewer of them because they're a problem for the nesting birds. My thought was that we should talk more to the biologists at the Hana Bird Refuge. I've heard they trap cats that get inside the fenced sanctuary and move them outside of it."

I frowned, turning this nugget over. "You think it's worth checking out? How could Lady Sapphire be caught up in something like that? She's a totally domesticated pet."

"Maybe it's worth talking to some folks who aren't Cat People," Keone said. "I don't know about you, but I'm getting interested in why all these feral cats are disappearing."

"Yeah, that bothers me, too," I agreed, forking up a mouthful of savory stir-fry and chewing thoughtfully. "But I think it's more likely Lady Sapphire was stolen so her kittens could be sold for profit. They are due on Christmas, leaving her owner alone on the holiday. Talk about a Grinch move. But I guess it can't hurt to find out more."

6

KEONE PUT my bike in the bed of his truck and took me home after our surf session. When I opened the door, Aunt Fae was in the kitchen and the whole house smelled like Christmas.

Keone brushed past me like a cookie-seeking missile and headed for the kitchen. "Auntie, whatchu got bakin'?"

"More holiday cookies." Aunt Fae was a no-nonsense sort of woman who wore jeans and flannels back home in Maine; she'd traded those in for shorts and tank tops here in the tropics, but over her usual casual garments today, she wore an apron I remembered from a dozen holidays growing up. Made of red and green cotton patchwork squares, the apron had been sewn for her as a girl by my grandmother, who was long gone. The sight of it, along with the rich smell of gingerbread, made my eyes prickle. For all the years I'd been in the Secret Service, Christmas was the one time Aunt Fae insisted I come home to visit, so I usually took two weeks of vacation to spend time with her in the depths of winter in Maine.

Now, we were together on Maui at the holidays for the first time, and even with the stress of Tiki being missing and my troubling new case, seeing how Auntie intended to keep all our traditions going warmed my heart cockles.

Keone headed for the counter where a row of gingerbread men was cooling on a rack. "Mind if I sample the goodies?"

"That's what they're there for," Aunt Fae said, smiling and accepting a kiss on her cheek as he helped himself to a large brown cookie. "Though I always say the frosting is the fun part on gingerbread."

I hugged Auntie as I reached for a warm cookie. "These are my favorite, frosting or no frosting!"

She mock-scolded us as Keone and I stuffed our faces with gingerbread. "You two must have been out surfing with those swimsuits and towels you're wearing," she said. "You should go get a shower and some warm clothes before you kids catch a chill."

"We're in Hawaii now. It's seventy degrees outside, at night in December." I pointed to Tiki's food bowl, currently filled with healthy kibble. "Where's Tiki? She usually eats at five p.m."

Auntie frowned, glancing at the metal dish as she opened the oven to check on her latest batch of cookies. "I refilled it for when she usually comes in. That's strange. Come to think of it, I haven't seen her all day."

Keone's and my eyes met. Both of our cheeks were bulging with gingerbread, but that didn't stop the cold finger of dread from tickling down my backbone. By his expression, he felt it too.

Keone chewed and swallowed with difficulty. "Kat. Is there something you aren't telling me? Where is Tiki?"

I grabbed a glass and filled it from the nearby carafe of filtered water. My throat had gone so dry I couldn't swallow the lump of gingerbread in my mouth.

A moment later I was able to say, "I don't know. She wasn't in bed with me this morning. I looked around but I thought she was outside, chasing birds like usual."

Aunt Fae shook her head and her silver bob shimmered like tinsel under the light above the stove. "She hasn't been hunting lately. Every time I see her, she's either eating or napping, so I don't think she's sick."

I forced a smile in my boyfriend's direction. "I'm sure her disappearance has nothing to do with our case, Keone."

Aunt Fae almost dropped the metal pan of cookies she'd removed from the oven; they were all the baked sections of a gingerbread house. "What's this investigation you're doing now, Kat?" Auntie set the pan down on the stovetop and turned to me, tugging off her padded oven mitts. "Sounds like something I should know about."

"We're looking for a missing cat. Not at all like Tiki." I rushed to fill in more details when Aunt Fae's face blanched. "A fancy, pedigreed Himalayan. Valuable. Probably stolen to obtain her upcoming purebred litter. Nothing like our girl. No one would steal Tiki, let alone be able to take her anywhere against her will."

I pictured Tiki's missing ear, her kinked tail, her homely patchwork calico body with her grumpy orange tabby face. Tiki was no beauty queen, and she was the size of a large raccoon.

"Yeah, but what about all those other missing cats we've uncovered while looking for Lady Sapphire?" Keone was reaching for another cookie when Auntie grabbed the edge of the counter for support. Fortunately, he was right beside her and caught her by the elbows as her knees crumpled. He helped her into a nearby chair as I rushed over.

"Oh my. I must've straightened up too fast and got dizzy," Aunt Fae said, brushing him off. "I'm a little overheated from the stove."

I fetched Auntie a glass of cool water, frowning at Mr. K over her head. "Take a load off and rest, Aunt Fae. You've been working too hard."

And maybe that's all it was, but I didn't like what I'd just seen happen with her. We needed to steer away from this stressful topic. "I wanted to tell you what a hit your fudge and cookies were with our mail delivery guy, Chad. He's been in a funk lately with such big loads to drive all the way out here, but when I gave him your plate of goodies today, he perked right up."

"Oh good." Auntie chugged from her water glass. "I'll make him some more treats ASAP."

"Yes, and Pua and I already decided to pass on most of the goodies customers drop off for us," I said. "The kid needs a little meat on his bones to deal with that drive and all the holiday boxes."

Throughout this exchange I observed Aunt Fae closely. Color was returning to her cheeks, and she stood up, grabbing a spatula to transfer the gingerbread house pieces to a cooling rack. "Do you have any leads on the missing cat you were hired to find?"

"Sadly, no." And there were a lot more than one missing feline. Even in the warm kitchen I shivered, tightening the towel around my body as I glanced out the uncovered windows into the darkness.

"But I've got us a meeting with the biologists at the Hana Bird Refuge tomorrow," Keone said. "Maybe we'll find out something useful about the anti-Cat People."

"There are anti-cat people here on Maui?" Aunt Fae frowned. "I'd want to know why."

"Feral cats, I should say," Keone clarified. "Truly wild felines are all over the island from the heights to the beaches, and they prey on critically endangered birds. Also, according to scientists monitoring the rare monk seals, female seals are dying from a disease carried by wild cats—and every female monk seal that dies also ends its family line. It's a serious problem."

Auntie blinked, frowning. "Feral cats are not a big deal in Maine. Eagles, hawks, and coyotes carry off any cats that aren't protected by their owners. I didn't realize what could happen in a place with no natural population safeguards like those predators."

"Sometimes the hunter becomes hunted in a place with a hierarchy of species," I said. "Hawaii is a different world, and from what I can tell so far, nature is in a delicate balance easily disrupted by outside creatures that are brought in. Even the plants are like that —new ones from elsewhere choke out the endemic species and throw everything off."

"Now you're getting life on a remote island," Keone said, looping his arms around my waist and resting his chin on my shoulder to look over at Auntie. "Want some help frosting those cookies? I volunteer as tribute."

Auntie laughed and I smiled and leaned into him, enjoying the warmth of his body. My old touchphobia still acted up with strangers, but since my relationship with Mr. K had deepened, I'd come to enjoy the occasional Public Display of Affection.

"Why don't you kids go take a shower and we'll decorate when you come back down?" Auntie reached for a bag of powdered sugar. "I'll get started on the icing recipe." She turned to wink at us. "Don't take too long, or I'll know what you're up to."

"We'll have to be quick then." Mr. K grinned and reached for my hand.

I let him tug me up the stairs, trying not to blush—but that was impossible. I was too new to this whole relationship deal not to feel self-conscious that my aunt guessed how we'd be soaping up when we stepped naked into the big walk-in with the rain shower fixtures.

But did that stop me from having bubbly fun with Mr. K once I got there?

Heck no.

I'd come a long way from my touchphobic past.

But later, after we'd decorated gingerbread cookies and Keone had gone home, Auntie and I took the golf cart abandoned by the New Ohia developers and drove around the artfully winding streets, calling for Tiki.

She never appeared.

Though my favorite stray had disappeared during the day plenty of times before, she always came home at night.

I had trouble falling asleep without Tiki beside me, and eventually had to take a sleeping pill to escape the worries that crowded my mind.

7

Dr. Malia Nama, the ornithologist in charge of the Hana Bird Refuge, was petite with long dark hair she wore down her back in a braid as thick as a man's wrist. Brown eyes sparkled behind round, wire-rimmed glasses as she gestured to the row of cages against one wall. "As you can see, we're nursing these birds back to health. We've put out a call to anyone finding an injured bird on this side of the island that we'll come pick it up and try to rehabilitate it."

The room Keone and I stood in the next day smelled strongly of guano, even though the cages appeared clean. I walked over, and the various seabirds inside, already against the back of their cages, tried to retreat further. "They seem so miserable."

"They are." Dr. Nama came to stand beside me next to one of the cages. "That's an 'A'o, or Newell's shearwater. It flew into one of the phone lines on the Hana Highway and got tangled." The bird's dark eyes gleamed in the dim light against her gray plumage set off by a white underbelly. The scientist pointed to the bird's wrapped leg and a close-cropped wing. "These birds are not used to humans, let alone being confined. But she's eating, and that's good. This breed is endemic to the Hawaiian islands, so while not on the endangered list, we watch their populations closely here on Maui since most of them live on Kauai."

"Do they nest out here?" Keone asked, joining them. "And are cats a problem for them?"

"Cats are absolutely a problem for shearwaters. The birds nest in burrows on the ground," Dr. Nama said. "The 'A'o was formerly a much more common bird with a wider breeding distribution throughout the Hawaiian chain. They have declined due to habitat loss and predation by introduced species such as cats, mongooses, rats, and barn owls." She pointed to the bird in question in her cage. "Young birds in particular are attracted to the lights of urban areas at night and many have collisions with power lines and buildings, like this female here. She is lucky to be alive."

I frowned. "Is there anything that can be done about that?"

"That's why the county has installed low-wattage, yellow lights along the highways. That's the best we can do, other than petition brightly lit events, like football games and such, to dim as soon as they're done with the lights."

"What do you do to protect the nests? And what do you do to monitor them?"

"Fences are our greatest friends in that particular effort." Dr. Nama pointed to a fluffy gray chick about the size of a grapefruit, huddled near a lightbulb in its cage. "See this sweet baby? One of our interns was monitoring its nest via video. He was able to save it from a cat that was carrying it off, but it was injured so we're keeping it here until it matures."

Interesting as this was, we needed to stay focused on our case, which involved missing cats, not birds. "Tell us more about what you do to deal with the predators."

"Well, inside the Refuge boundaries we trap them. Mongooses we release in the wild, away from the birds' nesting areas. Rats we euthanize. We don't do anything about the owls. And cats? We drive them to the Humane Society in Kahului. They are euthanized when they're not adoptable."

I shivered, thinking of Tiki. She would not have been adoptable under normal circumstances.

Dr. Nama eyed me, apparently noticing this. "There are also no-kill shelters on the island, but they prefer to focus on helping domesticated cats they can rehome."

"So what about those domestic cats? Ones with collars and owners. Do you ever catch them?" Keone asked, clearly steering us back to Lady's disappearance.

"Domesticated cats don't tend to wander so far out, all the way to the rugged areas where native birds are living. If they did, and we captured them, we'd still take them to the Humane Society so that their owners could find them there. The normal process with tame cats is to spay or neuter, rehome them if possible, and if not, return them to their community area." Dr. Nama sighed, turning her gaze to the cages of captive birds. "I don't like to see any animal harmed, but my concern is for our feathered friends. They are more vulnerable, and certainly rarer, than the cats on this island."

A man in a Hana Bird Refuge tee came in, carrying a cardboard box. "Hey, Dave." She turned to us. "This is our University of Hawaii intern, Dave."

Dave was a geeky-looking young guy with a large Adam's apple under a scruffy neck beard. He nodded as he set down a box that looked heavy on a pile of others.

"These two private eyes are looking for a missing cat. Seen any loose ones around our surveillance nest areas lately?" Dr. Nama asked him.

"Nope. And those ferals better not come around," Dave said. "I've got no love for bird killers." He patted a hip. "I'm armed against predators of our nesting area."

My attention sharpened on the Refuge's college intern, taking in hiking boots beneath combat style camouflage work pants covered with pockets that bulged with unknown tools. Nerdy as Dave was, he also appeared competent and strong. "Armed, how?"

"With the trusty childhood menace that I've finally found a

good use for." Dave took a serious looking Y-shaped slingshot with a rubber strap out of his back pocket. "Scares off mongooses too."

Dr. Nama shook her head. "We'd prefer to trap and move the predators. You know that, Dave. A slingshot's only temporary."

"Getting them to run off is better than nothing if we can't catch 'em," Dave said unrepentantly, and left.

Keone hurried after the guy, presumably to get his contact info or ask him more questions—and I was glad that my partner had taken the initiative on that. So far, we were working well together to cover all the bases.

I watched the fluffy gray chick with its big, awkward feet snuggle closer to the lightbulb. The poor thing was so little and helpless. "I can see how the birds are at risk from cats. But you also mentioned mongooses and barn owls as enemies."

"Yes. Mongooses in particular are a problem here on this island. That's why the shearwaters and other endangered ocean birds are gaining numbers on Kauai more than Maui and other islands. Kauai has no mongooses. They do have owls, but also not as many as we do."

"Hmm. Well, we're here because we're looking for a missing domesticated cat," I said. I scanned the room with its steel tables, microscopes, and computers, looking for—I didn't know what. Lady Sapphire clearly wasn't on the premises, nor likely had she ever been; but what about Tiki? "We've heard of a lot of feral cats suddenly going missing, as well as the domestic one we're hired to find. Have you captured any wild cats recently?"

"Happy to tell you we have not," Dr. Nama said. "We weren't able to catch the feral that grabbed this poor chick even. Short of trapping them using food, they're incredibly hard to capture."

I didn't know what to feel: happy that the cat got away from being caught and eventually put down? Or sad that the feline was still on the loose, trying to eat helpless endangered baby birds?

Either option sucked.

Dr. Nama must have seen the conflict on my face because she said, "It's a complicated issue, isn't it?"

"Yes, it is, but coming here to the Refuge has helped me understand the situation better. Thank you for that." I dug in my pocket and took out the card Keone and I had made up with K & K Investigations' logo on it and a work phone number, a burner cell I had agreed to lug around and keep charged for the business. I also handed over the missing cat flyer. "Here's our contact card and more info about Lady Sapphire, the cat we're looking for. If you could let your staff and volunteers know, we'd appreciate it."

"Of course. Thanks for coming in and taking the time to get to know what we do here, as well," Dr. Nama said graciously.

"I'm so glad I did. Now I know who to call if I ever see a bird in trouble."

Dr. Nama smiled and walked me to the front room of the little converted cottage where the Refuge's facility was located on the outskirts of Hana town.

Standing on the porch, Keone was staring at a bulletin board covered with informational flyers. He turned to me; his face was impassive and his brown eyes serious. There was no sign of Dave the intern. "Thanks for meeting with us, Dr. Nama."

"Please, call me Malia," she said, with a warm smile for my boyfriend. "I'll see you in the water."

"In the water? You must surf," I said.

"Sure do. That's how Keone and I met."

"Great. I'm learning, and I have a whole new respect for the sport." I forced a smile, suppressing a twinge of jealousy. Dr. Nama had a lot going on that I didn't—most especially, she shared Keone's heritage and culture. "Give us a call if you hear anything. Not just about Lady Sapphire, but any cats being captured."

"Will do," she said.

But as we went down the cottage's creaky wooden front steps, I wasn't sure the ornithologist would reach out. She had good reasons to want feral cats to disappear. I was glad I understood those reasons better, but I couldn't help thinking of Tiki in one of the square wire animal traps I'd glimpsed near the Refuge's rear door.

I waited until we were driving away, with me behind the wheel of the Ford SUV I'd nicknamed Sharkey, to broach the subject to Mr. K. "Do you think Dr. Nama will let us know if she comes across someone trapping cats?"

"Probably." Keone shrugged. "I'm more worried about that intern, Dave. Dave Finkelstein is his full name. I got his info in case we need to talk to him more. He's a University of Hawaii grad student in environmental biology, and he hates the feral cats. Makes no bones about it."

"Not good," I agreed. Tiki's distinctive, expressive face filled my mind. My cat's disappearance had made the situation personal. "I get why Bird People aren't fans after this, though. I'm beginning to see what a complex situation this is."

"Yep, it's Bird People versus Cat People. Speaking of the latter, I've set up a meeting for us in Kahului at the island's main no-kill cat shelter. We can share our info about Lady Sapphire and hear the other side of the story from a hard-core Cat Person, the retired vet in charge of The Cat Shelter."

"Sounds good. We need to grocery shop in town, anyway. Auntie's running out of baking ingredients. I'll get a list from her before we go." Kahului, Maui's biggest town, was a solid two hours away on a narrow winding road—but restocking food supplies was best done there as selection and prices were high of necessity at the tiny stores in Hana and Ohia. "Let's stop by my place before we go."

"And I can grab a few more of those gingerbread cookies," Mr. K said. "Fuel for the road."

I was on board with that grand idea, and also eager to find out the Cat People's side of the story.

8

ON THE DRIVE to the shelter in Kahului, winding around the "backside" of Maui with its open, rugged views, Keone and I decided to broaden our search in any and all interviews to include Tiki and the other missing cats in our area. It stood to reason that where one missing cat was, another might be.

So many felines disappearing at once couldn't be a coincidence.

We sped along the scenic highway with its grand vistas, rugged grassy slopes, and interesting twisted orange wiliwili trees as well as cinder cones. Eventually, turning right to head to Haleakala Highway, we arrived at The Cat Shelter, Maui's biggest no-kill nonprofit specializing in saving cats. The program was located in a fenced, open grassy field overlooking the valley below.

Keone got out and opened the cat-proof wire gate so we could drive in.

The Shelter consisted of a large property containing a couple of metal barns, a series of fenced pens, one great big cat cage surrounding a eucalyptus tree, and a simple modular home above. The whole property was the size of a residential block.

Keone took my hand as we exited the vehicle and greeted the Shelter's administrator, a rounded Caucasian woman with a jumble of shoulder-length hair in multicolored hues of green, pink, and blue. She wore teal-colored glasses and a purple tee emblazoned with the Shelter's logo, a pair of kittens whose profiles formed a heart.

"Thanks for making the time to see us," I said, holding out the flyer with Lady Sapphire's photo on it. "We're looking for this Himalayan specifically, and also some missing indoor-outdoor cats from our area of Hana and Ohia."

"I see." Dr. Jill Hanson, a retired veterinarian according to the Shelter's website, took the flyer, studied it, and put it on the clipboard she held. "So you're missing cats from East Maui, eh? We haven't had any from that area lately. In fact, we haven't had any new ones at all, recently."

"Is that a good thing? No news, I mean?" Keone was still holding my hand, and it had begun to feel claustrophobic. I detached gently and stepped away from him.

I was so much better with my touchphobia than I'd been. I had to take the wins I could, and hope he wasn't hurt by my ongoing need for physical and other kinds of space.

"Yes. No new cats are great. We're about bursting at the seams right now. I'm working with my volunteers on ways to get our babies out to new homes." Dr. Hanson pushed her glasses up with a finger, studying us.

"Where do the cats come to you from?" Keone asked.

"All over the island. Let me show you around." Dr. Hanson gestured for us to follow as she headed to the giant cage area. "Most of the cats we host are brought here by people who want to make sure they aren't euthanized for any reason. A lot of people come to Maui and adopt a pet, then have to leave for whatever reason. Or they find a stray who's not so pretty or friendly, and they want to make sure it finds a home. We make sure every cat has a home, even if it stays here forever." Her eyes flashed with passion as she looked at us over her shoulder—or maybe it was just the sun on her glasses. Either way, she meant her words. "Come see our main cat run."

She led us along a path of woodchips to the enormous chicken wire construction built around a tall eucalyptus tree that I'd noticed as we drove in. She opened a hasp-style wire door. "This is our main feline-friendly living area."

We followed Dr. Hanson inside the structure and were immediately swarmed by cats: black, white, calico, tabby, gray, orange, and every shade in-between. They'd mostly been lounging on a tall, carpet-covered wood structure erected around the bole of the tree; now they boiled down, and mewing and yowling and purring, surrounded us. Several wound their bodies around my legs. A couple put their paws up on my jeans to beg for pets.

I stood stock-still, feeling disloyal to Tiki that I wanted to grab up the chubby calico with the green eyes and long white whiskers. Or the sleek black male with tuxedo markings and white stocking feet. Surely Aunt Fae would understand.

But Tiki wouldn't, when she got home.

Hell had no fury like a jealous Tiki. She didn't just begrudge Keone his spot on our bed; she chased off any cat with the temerity to lay a paw on her turf. She'd eat these sweet kitties for breakfast if I brought one home.

"What a great place," I said, hands on hips as undulations of cats swirled around us in multicolored waves. I scanned for one-eared, tabby-faced calicos with kinked tails or blue-eyed, Himalayan princesses. "You certainly have a lot of them in here. Do they fight?"

As I asked that, a skirmish broke out in one corner. Keone ran over and clapped his hands, breaking up the hiss off.

"They're all spayed and neutered. Part of our services," Dr. Hanson said. "That keeps down most of the aggression, but there are some felines that came late to being surgically altered. They want to dominate and control their territories." She pointed to a large gray tabby Mr. K had shooed into a corner. The animal lashed its tail, its fur fluffed and eyes slitted, glaring at the rival who'd run away. "But generally they get along amazingly well. People do like you're doing. Come inside, hang out. See which one feels like a fit. And then take one or two home." She cocked her chin and smiled. "Maybe you want to bring a pair home to replace the ones you're missing."

The mere idea sent a shaft of grief through me. *Tiki was coming home!*

I shook my head. "Lady Sapphire is a valuable purebred, and my cat is . . . very territorial. But maybe Keone could bring his mom one for Christmas?" I was throwing my boyfriend under the feline adoption bus, but honestly what was one more when Ilima Kaihale had several already? "Your mom already has a few. Surely another would hardly . . ."

Keone shook his head regretfully. "The family has cut her off from getting any more. She loves them but can't keep them locked up inside, and they hunt the songbirds that come to her feeder and chase the neighborhood chickens. Myself, I don't have time for a pet with my work schedule, so I can't take one."

Dr. Hanson nodded. "I get it, but I have to try. So many beautiful cats, so few homes for them."

I was curious about what was inside the nearby barn. Though Dr. Hanson seemed honest and open, maybe our target animals were stashed away somewhere. "Can we tour the outbuildings, too?"

"Sure. One of the barns is primarily storage—the smaller one—but the other is where we keep cats in need of medical care and those that aren't socialized enough for the cat run."

"That's what you call this big cage?"

"That's what it is. They have room to run, climb, play, lounge. It's the closest thing to freedom that we can give them, and still keep them safe and contained."

"Safe?" My attention focused as we followed Dr. Hanson out, brushing cats off our legs and shutting the door behind us. "Safe from what? What is a threat to cats? I heard they have no predators in Hawaii."

"Humans. There are cat haters out there," she said darkly. "I'll say no more on the subject."

Dang it. She didn't want to vent about that, and it was an important line of inquiry for our cat hunt.

9

Dr. HANSON LED us to a door in the side of the large aluminum barn, and we stepped inside. The place smelled antiseptic, with a faint odor of feline musk. Eyes in all shades gleamed at us from rows of cages lining the dimly lit walls. "We keep the illumination low in here to let our sick animals rest more easily."

The cages were generous. None of the felines were cramped in their quarters, where beds, food, water, and litter boxes were clearly available. Many of the animals sported bandages or other evidence of medical intervention.

Dr. Hanson pointed to a framed-in room at one end of the barn whose entry was constructed of clear plastic panels. "There's my surgery. I perform spay and neuters here, and other surgeries as needed."

"Wow. This is impressive. And a big commitment for you," I said. "Are you the only staffer?"

"We have volunteers, but I'm the founder of The Cat Shelter, and only full-time employee. I never married or had children, so the cats are my family," she said matter-of-factly. "Everything I do is for them."

She was, indeed, a committed Cat Person. I didn't need to scan the cages to know that neither Tiki nor Lady Sapphire were inside. This woman wouldn't lie to us.

I glanced at Keone and met his gaze. He gave a slight nod and lift of his chin to the door; he was ready to leave.

But someone had taken all those missing cats we were looking for, and maybe Dr. Hanson knew something more about who, or what, made things unsafe for cats on Maui. She'd implied as much. "Can we talk a little more? Maybe in your office? I want to hear more about these haters you referred to."

Dr. Hanson's office was the front room of the single-story, simple modular home on the property we'd seen upon entry. Her desk faced the window at the front of the building. A view of the island spread out below in a panorama patchwork of former sugar cane fields, pastureland, the city of Kahului, and azure blue ocean on either side of Maui's narrow waist.

"I could sit at your desk and look at that view all day," I said, wrenching my gaze away to make eye contact with The Cat Shelter's founder.

"I was fortunate enough to buy this piece of land back in the 1980s when prices were more reasonable." She took a seat in the office chair behind her desk that faced a couple of chairs. Keone had already taken one, so I took the other.

"You asked about cat haters," she said. "I keep a file on those I suspect of doing real harm to cats."

Keone's brows shot up and we exchanged a surprised glance. "Are the police aware of this?" he asked.

"The police don't care," she said. There was no mistaking the bitter note in her voice. "And the animal control division is connected to the Humane Society here on the island. The officials on staff do go visit and investigate allegations of animal abuse, but when they remove a pet from an owner, it goes to their facility."

"Okayyy," I said, drawing out the word. "I'm sure everyone is doing the best they can given the challenges. Where do these 'haters' fit in?"

"They're conservationists. *Bird People.*" She spat the phrase like it tasted bad. "They blame cats for what's happened to the endangered native birds in Hawaii, but that's a big oversimplification. The problems begin with mosquitoes, climate change, and other predators—as well as cats."

Dr. Hanson explained that the colorful nectar-feeding native birds of Hawaii had been forced to the tops of the mountains because of mosquito-borne avian malaria. "Introduced species, like the mynahs, cardinals and doves, are immune to the malaria."

Keone leaned forward with his elbows on his knees, his brows drawn down. "We've talked with conservationists focusing on the endangered seabirds. They're aware of all the reasons the birds are in danger. They know cats are only one of several predators the birds have to contend with."

"But they blame cats more," she said. "I've heard someone in one of the conservation organizations is catching feral cats and shipping them away for medical research."

I sat back, startled. "This is news to us. Who did you hear this from?"

Dr. Hanson folded her lips into a tight line and shook her head. Her multicolored hair flew about like plumage; ironically her personal style was distinctly avian, not feline. "I don't want to get this person in trouble, and I don't have any proof. I shouldn't have said anything."

I leaned forward, imitating Keone's posture and his sincerity. "Listen. This is the first we've heard of such an evil thing, and if we could get to the bottom of this rumor—wouldn't that be good? We're professional investigators. We will do the work to get this stopped if it's happening, and you won't have to pay a dime or lose sleep over the possibility any longer."

Dr. Hanson's gaze darted to the phone resting on the desk beside her computer. "I need some time to think about that."

I knew when to leave once a seed was planted—clearly, she

wanted to call whoever had passed the rumor on to her—and I had a device that would ensure I knew the content of that call.

Trouble was, I'd left the darned Stingray device at home. Dang it! Not that it worked with landlines, anyway.

"Well, we understand. But would you be willing to share your file of 'haters' with us?"

"Not at this time." It was clear she'd shared all she was willing to.

I clapped my hands down on my thighs with an air of finality. "We'll wait to hear from you then. Let's go, Keone. We have other interviews to get to."

Mr. K gave me a subtle eye roll as he stood; the only stop we had left was a trip to the grocery store for baking supplies.

But I wanted it to seem like we had a lot of leads.

Which we didn't.

What we had was a ton of rumors about what *might* have happened to Lady and Tiki, and none of it was good.

We were headed out to Sharkey, getting ready to roll down to Kahului, when the work phone buzzed in my pocket.

We never got calls on the darned thing, but since we took the case, I'd been lugging it around. I removed it from my pocket to check—an unknown number. I didn't usually answer those, but I'd handed out a zillion flyers with the number on there and it behooved me to pick up. "Kat Smith with K & K Investigations," I said crisply.

Keone gave me a lovey-dovey look. I'd only read about those in romance novels; now I knew what one looked like. Apparently, it was "hot" when I sounded competent and in charge, or maybe it was hearing me say "K & K Investigations" that did it for him. Either way, Keone slid an arm around my waist and tried to distract me with a move that usually worked to rev my engine.

Unfortunately I couldn't enjoy it this time, because the voice on the phone, that of a gruff older man, spoke. "I have information about the missing cat."

I detached from Mr. K with a frown, holding up a finger. I walked to the car, opening the door, and sat down in the passenger seat. "You've called the right number to talk about the missing cat, sir. Can I get your name?"

Keone got in the driver's side but didn't start the engine as I made a gesture for a piece of paper and pen. He dug them out of the console and handed the items to me.

"I'm sorry. I don't want to tell you my name right now," the caller said.

"Okayyy," I said, much like I'd done with Dr. Hanson; it was super annoying to have people tease me with info and then not back it up. I put the phone on speaker so Keone could listen in. "What's this tip?"

"I saw a kid that works for that bird refuge in Hana driving around with a lot of chicken wire and lumber in his truck."

I exchanged a glance with Keone. That had to be Dave Finkel-stein, a known Cat Hater. "Tell us more."

"There isn't anything more."

I rolled my eyes. "Sir. What makes that suspicious?"

"The kid lives in a rental with no place to build anything. He's up to something." And then the guy ended the call.

I narrowed my eyes at Keone. "I have a feeling a lot of our tips might be like that. Random stuff. Rumors and suspicions."

Keone turned on Sharkey with a push of the Start button. "Yeah, but in this case it's worth checking out, and we know who that 'kid' is. I already told you I thought Dave was worth watching."

"You did."

We headed down Haleakala Highway in thoughtful silence, until the work phone rang again. I answered it on speaker. "This is Kat Smith with K & K Investigations."

"Hey, baby. I've seen you at the post office. I want to peel your clothes off like you were a tall sexy banana—"

I cut off the icky caller with a punch of my thumb. "Ew." I blocked the number.

"Banana, eh?" Keone slanted me a glance. "Interesting word choice."

Banana was our 'safe word' for when we needed a relationship discussion. We hadn't had to use it in a good long while.

"Yeah, that is odd." But I didn't have time to get into it anymore when the phone rang again.

Once more, I picked up, greeted, and put the person on speaker. The caller, a woman, and a local resident by the cadence of her voice, refused to give her name. "I don't know if this is useful, but I saw two young girls at Ohia General Store buying cat food. Girls that don't have a cat."

I digested this for a moment. "Um. Maybe they have a cat now?"

"If they do, they shouldn't."

I thought of Sandy and Windy Nakasone, two girls who were often unsupervised due to family circumstances. The village of Ohia looked out for them as a community, but Windy had a crush on Mr. K, and had warned me off dating him. To no avail, obviously.

"Can you tell me the girls' ages? Names?"

"Never mind." The caller hung up.

Keone was the one to roll his eyes this time. "Ho, da humbug."

I loved it when he used Hawaiian creole dialect, also known as 'pidgin.' "Yep. That was clear as mud. If this is what cops go through with tip lines . . ."

"We do have a little something to follow up on. I'll try to find out what Dave was up to if you find out about the mysterious girls buying cat food."

I knew the owner of Ohia General Store—Opal Pahinui. She and her husband were some of my closest friends, in fact. Surrogate parents, even. Opal would remember any girls buying cat food from her little mercantile, and we were overdue for a catch-up visit, anyway.

"I thought you'd like an excuse to visit Opal and Artie," Keone said, and twinkled his pretty brown eyes at me.

"And you'd be right." I batted my navy blues right back at him. "Good division of labor. K & K Investigations is running great so far."

"Now if we could just solve our first case."

"Yep." That was sobering. We really weren't making much progress on finding Lady so far, let alone Tiki.

We eventually pulled up in front of Costco in downtown Kahului. I set up a voicemail on the work phone to screen the ridiculous calls we were getting, and then we grabbed a cart and plunged into the chaos of shopping at Maui's only mega superstore during the holiday season.

10

THE NEXT MORNING I went for an early morning lap swim with the turtles in Ohia Bay. Humpback whales, here in the islands for their annual birthing and breeding festival, tail-slapped and breached in the ocean outside the bay, while a rainbow trailed down from a cloud.

All of it was going on at once in an over-the-top episode of Hawaii awesomeness that couldn't banish the worried blues I was experiencing about Tiki's ongoing absence.

Wrapping in my towel, I headed over to Opal and Artie's market. Ohia General Store was a little mercantile with a big porch right next to the post office and across the street from the beach, which had helped our friendship deepen in the months I'd been in Ohia.

As was their custom on a Sunday morning, my dear senior friends were seated on their porch before opening the store. Opal popped up from her chair as soon as she saw me coming up from the beach wrapped in a towel. "Kat! I've been seeing your missing cat flyers all over town. How is the investigation going?"

"Got any malasadas or coffeecake?" My tone was leaden. "I need carb therapy."

Artie, blind but very good at navigating his world, was also an exceptional musician. He gave the strings of his acoustic guitar a dramatic strum. "That does not sound like it's going well."

"As a matter of fact, it's not." I flopped into Opal's vacated chair. "I want to drown my sorrows."

"On it." Opal, who read runes on the side and loved to dress the part, wore a red holiday scarf held in place with a rhinestone reindeer pin, complete with a pulsing, light-up nose. "But you can't tell Artie anything about what's going on until I get back with your breakfast." She hurried off into the depths of the building.

Artie leaned over to me, smiling conspiratorially. "Breakfast? It's more like sugar, spice, everything nice, and a cup of coffee to chase it down," he said. "Calling it breakfast is a bit of a stretch." Artie had diabetes, and keeping his blood sugar under control was an ongoing challenge as he was the cook for the store's ready-to-eat treats.

"I don't care. I need all the feel-good chemistry I can get."

Artie's bushy brows drew together in concern. "This sounds like it's gotten personal."

"It has, and I'll tell you why when Opal gets here again." I leaned back in the chair, tightening the towel around myself. I shut my eyes and tried to relax as Artie broke into an acoustic guitar version of "Silent Night."

Opal soon reappeared with a holiday-themed paper plate loaded down with a pile of tasty malasadas that a local bakery delivered every Sunday, along with a giant square of delicious-looking cinnamon covered coffeecake, still steaming from baking, a pat of butter melting in the middle of it. "You came at the perfect time, I just pulled this out of the oven."

I stuffed one of the haupia coconut pudding filled malasadas into my mouth and chewed as I waited for the gently steaming cake to cool. "Mmm," was all I could say, for a good long minute. "Mmm-hmm." I chased the pastry down with fresh Kona coffee and then dug my fork into the moist, buttery coffeecake. "Yep. I needed this."

After a few bites had taken the edge off of my craving and Artie's mellow music, along with Opal's maternal, completely accepting gaze had soothed my emotional upset, I was ready to tell them what the real problem was. "It's not just that fancy cat Lady Sapphire that's missing. Tiki is gone too. I haven't seen her in three days."

Opal gasped, covering her mouth with a hand.

Artie stilled the strings of his guitar and cupped a meaty brown hand around his ear. "Say that again?"

I repeated it, the delicious food turning to ash in my mouth. I shoveled more in anyway and gagged it down with a slurp of coffee. Comfort eating was one of my go-to stress relievers, but this meal meant I would have to take an extra jogging lap around new Ohia this evening. That was no hardship since I planned to go looking and calling around the park for Tiki again.

Opal unfolded one of the guest camp chairs and sat in it as if her knees had given out. "Tiki would never leave you on her own."

"I don't know. Tiki's a cat, after all. She does what she wants." My lips felt numb, and I had to make them move. I drank more coffee, staring at the crumbled cake on my plate.

When you opened your heart and let people or animals in, they disappeared and left you alone, cold, lonely, and scared . . . just like my parents had when they died in the accident with me in the car when I was nine. They'd died and gone to heaven, leaving me to freeze to death in the snowbank that killed them.

I had developed my touchphobia after being unconscious in that car for hours until I was rescued by first responders using the Jaws of Life. Somehow the rough grip of that rescue by the paramedics had caused me to associate human touch with loss and trauma.

I was always trying to protect myself from the next time something bad would happen . . . until I'd moved to Ohia and come to believe the price of keeping my heart closed was too high.

So I'd lowered my guard, and now look what had happened. My beloved cat was gone, leaving me to mourn her.

Inevitably, I thought of Keone.

Mr. K.

My boyfriend, with the twinkly brown eyes, great body, smart mind, and many skills. He was even a good investigator and partner.

I had said the L word to him.

He was bound to dump me.

Opal snapped her fingers in front of my face, and I realized she had already done that several times. "Let's go inside. We can't open the store until I read the runes and see what they have to say about all this."

Normally I loved when Opal read the runes. I was fascinated with her process, a combination of intuitive interpretation and symbology that used an ancient form of communication to bring messages from the beyond.

But not today. "I just want to be left here with my carbs." I pulled my plate closer and embraced it. "I'm fine. It's fine."

"Nope." Opal shook the pocket of her pants, and I heard the familiar rattle of the kukui nut shells from which she'd made her personal set of Nordic runes. "A reader always keeps their totems close to their body, to absorb their personal energy," she told me once, when I asked her why she always carried them in her pocket. "And serious rune readers make their own set. No commercial set can quite capture dynamic energy like a person's own creation."

Artie stood up, tucking his guitar under his arm. He took my elbow in his big hand. "Come on, Kat. Bring your breakfast and you can eat it in the kitchen. We need to tune in and see what the universe has to say about all this."

Opal picked up my plate. "Can't you tell she's reliving her trauma?" She told her husband. "We need to support her."

The idea of these two elders supporting me, a strapping six foot one woman in the prime of her life . . . but of course, they meant emotionally. The two of them wrapped their arms around me, one on either side, and walked me through the store after Opal paused to hang up the OPENING LATE TODAY sign on the door.

"Our customers will have to wait," she said. "Kat needs us more."

The Pahinuis' apartment was located through a door behind the checkout counter. On the other side of the door, a pass-through storage area lined with shelves of supplies for quick stocking was a favorite haunt of Artie's; he kept a comfy armchair there. Beyond that, a locked door marked PRIVATE guarded their living realm.

Opal unlocked that portal, and we stepped into a warm, colorful kitchen, redolent of cinnamon and baking.

The smell shocked me out of my weird funk. "This reminds me of our house," I said. "Aunt Fae is baking up a storm now that Keone and I brought her fresh supplies from Kahului when we were in town on the investigation."

"You can tell us all about it after I read the runes for this situation," Opal said. "But for now, I don't want to know anything besides the fact that Tiki is missing."

I sat down like a bag of dropped rice at the couple's humble Formica table. Artie went to the stove and cut himself a generous piece of coffeecake, shoveling it onto a plate and adding a fork.

Apparently, I wasn't the only one in need of carb therapy.

And for once, Opal didn't remind him about his blood sugar; she was too busy settling herself at the table, having dumped the contents of the rune pouch into her hand.

Once Artie was seated with his coffeecake, Opal took off her festive red velour scarf and spread it on the table. Without further ado, she shook the handful of kukui nut shells into her cupped fingers so that they made a musical sound as they moved. She breathed on them and tossed the shiny black totems onto the cloth.

By some quirk of physics, two of them rolled off the table and bounced onto the floor.

Opal's pale blue eyes sought mine. "As we often see, there are runes that don't want to be counted in a reading."

I nodded. We had noticed that this often seemed to happen, even though Opal used the scarf's soft surface to try to corral all of the symbols from getting away.

Opal removed a pair of reading glasses from her front pocket and slid them onto her long nose. She peered through them at the reading, muttering to herself. Finally, she prodded one shiny black shell that lay on top of another with a fingertip. "This one is fortuitous. This is the rune of spring, and life, and new beginnings. It is topmost on this reading. A very good sign."

I straightened up a little.

While the runes were often vague or confusing, the gist or general tone of the readings seemed to come true. I found reassurance, a question, or a caution in what she interpreted.

Opal pointed to another of the shells. "This is the one we need to watch out for. It's a warning. Loss and grief and a hard season are at hand." She got up abruptly and searched a nearby drawer for her drawing book.

I was familiar with her process: after tossing the runes, she often sketched her discovery, and later shared closer or more detailed interpretations. When I asked why she didn't just take a photo of the casting, she'd said that the organic process of drawing what she saw helped her uncover deeper meaning.

"What I notice overall here is a time of testing. A time of worry and grief, and of confronting old wounds," she said.

I shivered, flashing once again to my parents' death and all my past issues. It had taken my dedicated Aunt Fae, Keone's patient love, a passionate, crazy cat named Tiki, and a quirky Hawaii village to begin to heal me.

Even so, I could still return to a dark place easily, and right now I was tempted to stay there as I considered the loss of my beloved pet.

Artie set his big, warm hand over my cold one as it rested on the table. His gentle touch, instead of repelling me, grounded me in my body and reminded me of the present rather than sending me into the past. "We're here for you, Kitty Kat."

Opal met my gaze and smiled. "This is, overall, a very hopeful reading. Yes, there is darkness here. Worrisome things are afoot. Grief and sorrow are a theme. But so are happiness and new beginnings."

"And if that's not what the first Christmas was about, I don't know what is," Artie said. "After all, we're celebrating the birth of a child, born long ago and far away in a manger."

"Yeah, we forget that's the original story in all the hustle and bustle of Santa and elves and reindeer," I agreed. I wasn't religious, but I've always loved the story of baby Jesus's birth, how the animals, wise men and shepherds worshiped a humble infant King as He lay in a manger with His loving parents and the bright star of the east shining over the scene.

I sat tall and rolled my shoulders back. "Thanks so much for all of this, Opal. Artie, you too." I turned my hand over to grasp his. "I don't know what I'd do without you both."

"You'd cry and be sad, and then you'd be fine," Artie said. "It's the way of things." His wisdom made my eyes prickle.

"And then you'd run off and shag that hunky pilot of yours," Opal said.

"You're both right—but the upshot is I'm glad to have you two in my life." I picked up my fork and dug into my delicious breakfast. "After this I'm going surfing with Mr. K to burn off these calories. The day is bound to get better."

Opal smiled at me. "That's the spirit, Kat. The universe has a way of balancing things out. Even in the darkest moments, there's hope for a new beginning."

I finished eating as Artie tuned his guitar, filling the room with soft holiday melodies. I closed my eyes and let the music wash over me, feeling the warmth of the kitchen and the love of my friends surround me.

Opal gathered up her runes and placed them in their pouch. "I think that's enough for today," she said. "We've gotten a good sense of what's to come, and now it's up to us to face it with courage."

I nodded. "I won't stop looking until I find all of the missing cats."

As we said our goodbyes and I walked out of the Pahinuis' apartment, I took a deep breath of sea-laden morning air and felt a surge of energy. "Time to go surfing and get a fresh perspective."

I pep-stepped over to Sharkey the SUV, parked at the beach; but it wasn't until I was well on my way to Koki Beach and meeting Mr. K that I remembered—I hadn't asked Opal about the girls who'd been seen buying cat food in the store.

11

AFTER SURFING, which did what I'd hoped it would to restore my emotional state, Keone put my board on his racks and then handed me a clean, warm towel from behind his seat.

We wrapped up, smiling at each other as we leaned against his truck because . . . well, we liked doing that. He was scrumptious and looked at me like I was, too.

But I still had angst going on. "Banana."

"Ah, the relationship safe word." He smiled. "Lay it on me, baby. Let's talk it out."

I sucked in a breath, blew it out. "I'm waiting for you to dump me. It's inevitable."

Keone straightened up. "What?"

"Yeah. All good things come to an end. Usually suddenly. Like Tiki going missing." Tears fogged my eyes. "I can't take the suspense. Break up with me already."

Keone didn't say anything, and I couldn't see him through the water in my eyes. I dashed the moisture away and blinked until he came into focus. "What? Say something."

"I'm wondering what the heck brought this on. What did I do?" His voice was low and rough, and he reached out to pull me close, his arms wrapping around my damp, towel-covered back. He stroked my surf-tangled hair. "I'm not breaking up with you. Period."

"I want to believe you, but it's hard." I swallowed the lump clogging my throat. "I have issues."

"I know you do. What would it take for you to believe I mean to stick around and make things work, no matter what?" Mr. K set me back a bit so that we made eye contact. "I love you, Kat. Even if you're a little bit nuts. Which is okay because I am too."

"I don't know," I said miserably, staring down at my sandy feet. "I'm better at planning a defensive tactical strategy than having a relationship."

"Those days are behind you. How about I show you how I feel since talking isn't working." He pulled me in for a kiss. That went on for a bit and pretty soon I forgot what I'd been worried about.

Eventually I detached and cleared my throat. "How's your part of the investigation going?"

"I called Dave Finkelstein and left a message asking about the chicken wire spotted in his truck. He hasn't returned my call," Keone said, rubbing his shiny black curls with his towel. "I'm planning to drop in on his house next."

"Okay. Well, I forgot to ask Opal about the girls buying cat food when I went by there. Got distracted by her doing a rune reading. Signs were hopeful," I said, and told him about my morning. "What're you up to for the rest of the day?"

"I've got to try to catch Dave at home and find out about that chicken wire. After that, some Christmas decorating and prep to do with Mom," he said. "We're getting ready for the big holiday luau with all the family that we do every year on Christmas Eve. I hope you and your auntie will come?" He twinkled his eyes at me.

I tried to twinkle at him too, but it probably looked like I had a bug in my eye because he laughed.

"Sure we'll come," I said. "A real Hawaiian luau holiday feast? Wouldn't miss it. Aunt Fae and I have our own tradition, but it's on

Christmas Day. It involves stockings, presents, eating the ginger-bread house we made, and lying around reading new books we bought each other, which we always exchange as gifts. I hope you'll join us for any part of it."

"I'm in, especially for the eating, lounging and presents," Keone said.

"Then you have to come help build the gingerbread house," I told him. "We do it a few days ahead so it's still fresh enough to eat."

We got our phones out and booked our holiday activities in our calendars, then engaged in a kiss that tasted of hope and the sea.

"That will tide me over until I see you again," he whispered. "I'm glad we're sharing the holidays. It means a lot to me—and my family."

I felt a quiver of intimidation.

The Kaihales were a very big, very noisy, very opinionated, and very curious family. Keone had seemingly hundreds of aunts, uncles, and cousins along with two brothers, both married with offspring. The clan had welcomed me, but there were still moments when I felt like an outsider "fresh off the plane." Maybe that would always be the case.

I had to focus on the positive: his mother Ilima liked me, from what I could tell. She'd given me a lei at a party. She'd loaned me her bike. She'd poured my offering of vodka into the family's punch bowl at dinner one night. And hopefully, she'd accept what Aunt Fae and I brought to the luau, and we'd be a part of things. "I'm glad, too. Christmas is going to be great."

But as I waved and got into Sharkey, I thought of Tiki—and poor Mrs. Scarborough, all alone.

How great could the holiday be, without our cats?

I WENT HOME and took a shower, then called Opal at the store. "I forgot to ask you something about the investigation," I said. "We had a tip line call that some girls were in the store buying cat food —girls who don't have a cat."

"What?" Opal sounded distracted. "I've got a customer here. Just a minute." She hung up.

I dragged a comb through my long, wet hair as I sat in the bay window, staring out at the grassy hill behind the house.

Still no Tiki.

Where could she have gone?

The thought of the different ways there were for a cat to come to harm made me cold with fear. I was about to hop up and pace the room when my phone rang with a call from Opal.

"The great thing about this tablet and scanner wand I use is that all the purchases are in here," she said. "Yep, a five-pound bag of cat chow went out a few days ago, all by itself. But I didn't ring it up; I wasn't working that afternoon. Your Aunt Fae handled that purchase."

I'd almost forgotten Aunt Fae had a part-time job working at the Ohia General Store, because she was usually there when I was at the Post Office.

"Thanks, Opal, it's great you could find that out so easily. Hopefully Auntie will remember who bought the cat food." I paused, tapping my lips with a finger. "Did you have any more thoughts about the reading this morning?"

"Nope. The thing to remember is that, overall, the runes were positive."

"You're right," I said with forced cheer. "Happy holidays, dear friend."

"Back atcha. And don't worry about Tiki. She's a survivor. She was living off the land and getting by fine before you came to town. She'll come home, waving that kinked tail, sometime soon. Artie told me this morning he woke up after seeing it in a dream."

Artie had a prophetic gift too, but it involved flashes of insight. "That's the first time I've heard of him having a dream about something."

"It doesn't happen often, so we pay attention when it does," she said. "Let me know how things go with the cat hunting!"

"Will do." I ended the call and slid the phone into my pocket. Artie's dream was hopeful, at least.

I headed downstairs and smiled at the sight of neat rows of macadamia nut powdered sugar balls, lined up in rows on newspaper all over the counter.

Over in the living room, Aunt Fae was sound asleep in a rattan chair, her feet up on the ottoman, her head tipped back. Soft snores added a backbeat to the holiday tunes jingling about the kitchen emitted by the old-fashioned antenna radio I remembered from my youth.

I had a nice surprise gift for Auntie—a new speaker that would play music off her phone, complete with a music app that I'd bought a whole year's subscription for. She was going to love not having to listen to static and commercials.

Popping a macadamia nut ball into my mouth, I savored the treat as it both crunched and melted. I washed it down with a glass of cold milk.

My gaze fell on Tiki's full food bowl, reminding me she was still gone.

The cookie turned to lead in my belly.

I approached, and gently shook Aunt Fae's shoulder. "Auntie? I have a question for you. It's important."

12

AUNT FAE SAT up and shook her blunt bob. Her thick silver hair flew around and settled; it looked great considering she trimmed it herself every month. "Just resting my eyes for a minute, honey. What was it you wanted?"

I nudged her feet, clad in green and red striped socks, to the side so I could sit on the ottoman in front of her. "I heard you sold a bag of cat food to a couple of girls who are not known to have a cat. I was wondering if you remembered anything about them."

Auntie knuckled her eyes and put her feet on the floor, then stood up with the grace and strength of a younger person. She stretched her arms overhead, bending backward, then forward to touch her toes. Finally she straightened up and put her hands on her hips, meeting my gaze. "Yes. What I remember is that those girls looked like they needed a bath and a good meal themselves and shouldn't be spending the little money they had on a cat."

I knew who the girls were immediately: Sandy and Windy Nakasone, eight and nine years old. They'd lost their mother in the last year and their father, depressed and struggling with grief, worked in Kahului and was seldom home. Their aunt Lani lived with them, supposedly helping supervise the girls, but she wasn't often around either—she had long shifts at the Hotel Hana as a waitstaff, especially during the holidays.

"Anything else you can remember?"

She tipped her head, looking up and to the left. "They both had long black hair that needed a good brushing. I asked them what kind of cat they had; I was trying to be friendly and make conversation. They said they didn't have a cat. When I asked where their parents were, the younger one made a very rude hand gesture and told me to mind my own business."

A horrible suspicion filled my mind—*could the girls be out of food, and reduced to eating kibble?*

I'd heard desperate people sometimes used cat or dog food as a protein source, but the idea of little girls having to do so turned my stomach. "Thanks, Auntie. Can I get some of your cookies? I have to go visit someone in Old Ohia."

"Sure. I made up some platters already." She went over to our pantry and opened it. "Grab any of these and pass them on when you want to spread holiday cheer."

Each festively printed cardboard plate was piled high with a variety of tasty cookies and then wrapped in transparent red cellophane. I took two platters. "Great. I'll try not to steal any. How do you feel about attending Keone's family's luau on Christmas Eve?"

"Excited," Auntie said instantly. "Ask them what we should bring."

I grinned. "That's what I hoped you'd say. I won't be gone long."

I took the golf cart we'd inherited with the house as the thing was charged and ready to go. With the wrapped cookies on the passenger seat, I drove through the park and out the pretty rock waterfall gate with its sign that had been converted to read "NEW OHIA STATE PARK" in gold letters.

I trundled in the golf cart for a brief and harrowing few moments down narrow, busy Hana Highway with its streams of tourists. I gritted my teeth and pushed the pedal to the floor, soon turning into the dirt parking lot in front of the Ohia General Store with a sigh of relief and a honking of horns.

Artie took up Opal's spot behind the counter with his assistive technology scanner to do checkouts after I arrived at the store in the golf cart to talk to Opal about what I had discovered from Aunt Fae.

Opal went into action as soon as she heard my theory about the cat food. "It's been a while since we took groceries over there. Let's grab some things and take them over together, along with your cookies," she said. "That ought to get them to talk."

We loaded the grocery bags on the cart and got in, drove across the lot, and turned up Hibiscus Street. As usual, the little town was quiet on a Sunday afternoon.

The girls' house was not far down Plumeria Street, midway up the slope to the top of the hill crowned by a church and graveyard that defined the highest point of Ohia.

A patchy, weed-choked lawn led to a small older plantation style home, as most of them were in Ohia—but this home spoke of the family's financial and time struggle through peeling paint and a sagging porch.

"Their father works in construction," Opal said, glancing around at the neglect. "You know the old saying: it's the cobbler's children that go barefoot."

"Actually, I haven't heard that one," I teased. "What's a cobbler got to do with bare feet? I thought it was a tasty baked dish, usually made with peaches, but sometimes around here, with mango."

Opal rolled her eyes as we pulled up the girls' driveway. We got out of the cart. I walked behind Opal, holding the two plates of Christmas treats stacked in one hand and a bag of groceries in the other, as she led the way up onto the porch. Two small pairs of battered rubber slippers beside the mat told us that the girls were home.

Opal knocked on the front door's splintery frame.

Almost immediately, it opened. The older girl, Sandy Nakasone, stared at us from behind an interior screen door. Her expression softened as she took in the bags of groceries we held, and she broke into a smile when she saw the cookies. "Aunty Opal, and Ms. Smith from the Post Office. Hi."

"Sandy, we thought you might need a few things for your holiday. Can we come in?" Opal asked.

Immediately, Windy, who had crowded in behind her, piped up. "No! We need to do some cleaning first."

I wanted to overrule this, but Opal gave me a tiny head shake. "I heard you girls bought some cat food at my store," she said, as she handed Sandy the bag of groceries when the girl opened the door. "So I put another bag of food in here. Did your family adopt a kitty?"

"I don't know who you were talking to," Windy said in her surly way. She snatched the bag of groceries out of my hand. "We like to feed the mynah birds in our backyard. They love cat food."

This had a rehearsed sound to it, and nobody in this area encouraged the mynahs to hang around and be fed. They were as voracious and aggressive as crows were in Maine.

Windy must've seen the skeptical expression on my face because she put her little fists on her hips. "What?" she barked aggressively.

"Nothing." I held out the two plates of cookies, one stacked on top of the other. "My aunt made these for you. Don't eat them all at once, or you'll make yourself sick."

"Like you care." Windy snatched the treats and spun around, walking away into the depths of the house. The screen door banged as she let it fall behind her.

Sandy smiled tentatively at us. "Windy misses our mom a lot at this time of year."

"I bet she misses your mom any time of year," I said. "I lost both my parents when I was around your age. It never really stops hurting, I'm sorry to say."

Sandy's face fell; clearly, she was hoping things would get

better. Opal elbowed me in the ribs. "Time heals all wounds," she said briskly. "Don't believe everything you hear. But in the meantime, where are your dad and your Aunt Lani?"

"They're working, as usual." Sandy's expression was wooden, shut down.

My attempt to form a bond had definitely backfired. I was clearly no good with kids. Removing myself was the best idea. "Let us know if you need anything. Anything at all," I said. "You know where to find me at the post office." I turned on my size eleven Nikes and went to the golf cart.

Opal stayed in the doorway, talking to Sandy for several more minutes. I sat in the cart, miserable. I'd rubbed salt in the poor girls' wounds.

Opal returned, I put the cart in reverse, and we rolled down the driveway in silence.

"I wish I hadn't said that to them. I meant . . . they're not alone. In that loss." My voice trailed off.

Opal put a soft hand on my arm. I glanced down to see her knuckles, gnarled with arthritis, through a blur.

"I know you meant well, Kat. Sandy knows it too. So does Windy, even though she's not ready to stop being mad at everybody. What you said was good, you said something real, while I told them 'time heals all wounds.'" Opal shook her head. "When we both know it doesn't. I was able to modify our *faux pas* a little bit, by proposing an idea to take a wreath up to their mom's memorial plaque at the cemetery. Maybe you want to come with us?"

"I don't think they would want me there," I said. "Especially Windy." Windy had a crush on Mr. K. She had warned me off of dating him several times and made her dislike of me clear.

"Maybe you're right. I'll get the wreath and make sure something special is done for their mother on Christmas Day."

I blinked the moisture from my eyes, but too late. I sideswiped a trashcan that had been left out, sending it sprawling into the street with a clatter.

"Nice driving!" I heard in Windy's piping voice, followed by hollow laughter.

Without a word, I stopped the cart, got out, righted the trashcan and put the lid on it.

Windy Nakasone was free to mock me if it made her feel better, but I sure wasn't buying the story that the girls were feeding cat food to the mynah birds in their backyard.

13

THE FOLLOWING WEEK FLEW BY.

If that sounds like Keone and I let the investigation drop, we didn't. But both of us had full-time jobs with required hours to keep, so it was hard to pursue the negligible leads we had in the busy last week before Christmas.

Keone made his surprise drop-in to Dave Finkelstein's bachelor pad, a funky old house in Hana with all its rooms rented out to different single dudes. The guy refused to tell him anything about the chicken wire reported seen in his truck. End of that clue.

Meanwhile, I snuck by the Nakasone girls' place on Plumeria Street twice after work, tiptoeing around their cottage on my size elevens and trying to catch a glimpse of whatever animal they might be feeding cat food to.

Nothing, and no one, was visible behind or around their house; although the mynah birds *were* extra friendly and squawked excitedly when they saw me. Maybe they did get some of the kibble and associated humans with food.

The phone tip line was a bust. All the messages I retrieved were strange ramblings from lonely people, or rude, wannabe sexy messages from creeps. Lei had told me that was par for the tip line course.

So, by the end of Saturday, I was frustrated getting ready for the Red Hat group's annual holiday celebration held on the porch of the Ohia General Store. I donned a purple sweatshirt and the gaudy rhinestone-spangled scarlet ball cap a Red Hat member had made for me. With Aunt Fae in tow, we headed out to join the other Red Hatters for their party.

Hawaii's version of winter had arrived with temps that were a bit cooler, bigger surf and frequent rain showers, along with shorter days—though the state had been spared the annoyance of time changes. Aunt Fae and I took Sharkey to stay dry in case one of those showers moved through.

When we arrived, we saw that Opal had put her wooden fold-open sign out by Hana Highway to discourage tourists from turning into the lot. It read:

"*RED HAT SOCIETY CHRISTMAS!*
Store closed. Private Party.
Keep driving!"

Even so, many a rental car slowed with its carload of rubber-necking tourists as they considered turning in and crashing what looked to be a festive event. I pulled into the parking lot and savored the feeling of being in the group; the Red Hats had been a big part of making my transition to life in Ohia a success.

Our small local Red Hat Society had shrunk in size by one prominent member when that person had been arrested. The remaining ladies had made a determined effort to widen the group's membership by each pledging to bring a possible new recruit to the holiday gathering.

My prospect was Aunt Fae, who had never officially joined the Society but considered herself an honorary member. After months in Ohia, she was ready to take the plunge and make it official, and I was happy to have her at my side.

We parked in front of the shack beside the post office, leaving room for the pop-up tent off the verandah of the store that Opal had set up to increase the party space. Holiday music tinkled from a boom box set on the railing, and a red and green clothed table groaned with food and two large punch bowls at one end of the porch.

"Isn't this festive!" Aunt Fae exclaimed, getting out of the SUV, and picking up a tray of her now famous holiday cookies. "And it's so fun to not have to deal with the cold. I'm not over being outside in December."

"Me too." I shut the car door behind us. "The Red Hats always have such good food. Wait 'til you taste Pearl's Japanese treats. She usually brings something special."

Josie and Edith, two of my favorite Red Hats, pulled up and parked beside us in Josie's VW van. Seated in the rear, Edith's daughter Lola and another woman were engaged in animated conversation.

I was astonished to see Lola as Edith's guest; the middle-aged woman with her bleached blonde hair had gone to jail in connection with a murder scheme involving Edith and me.

14

EDITH MUST HAVE SEEN my wide eyes and dropped jaw, because she hopped out of the van and hurried straight over to me. My friend's short, barrel-shaped body was packed into a bright purple tube dress embellished with glittering spangles. Her favorite red hat, a witch-style topper, was wrapped for the occasion in blinking colored lights.

"I hope you don't mind that I brought Lola. She's out early, and she's sober," Edith said quickly. "We've been going to family counseling, and . . ."

"Say no more," I said. "Lola may have taken a couple of potshots at me, literally, but I know she didn't have any real malice toward me."

Lola'd definitely had murderous intent concerning her mother, though. I didn't mention that. If Edith was ready to forgive and forget, who was I to argue?

Aunt Fae stepped forward and stood at my side as Lola, dressed in one of Edith's borrowed purple outfits, exited the van, and helped her friend out to join us. The statuesque black woman beside Lola sported a tall, braided hairdo topped by a tiny, sparkling red bowler. She smiled brightly and approached us, arm in arm with Lola.

"Welcome to Ohia," I said, extending a hand. "I'm Kat. This is my Aunt Fae. And you are?"

"Betty," the woman said, shaking my hand. Her nails were long and painted iridescent purple. "I'm Lola's sponsor in her sobriety program. We're here, in no small part, for her to make amends."

Before I could brace myself for the physical contact, Lola threw her arms around me and squeezed. "I'm sorry," she said, her voice muffled in the chest of my purple sweatshirt.

I clenched my teeth and held my arms rigidly down at my sides with an effort. My touchphobia was totally activated by being grabbed by a former hostile. It was all I could do not to fling Lola off, preferably onto her back with my foot on her neck.

"I didn't mean to shoot you," Lola went on, squeezing me again. "I was drunk."

"But you did shoot at me. Twice," I said stiffly. "I'm lucky to be alive."

"I apologize," Lola echoed. "I won't do it again."

"Glad to hear that." I flexed my arms, so she was forced to let go, and detached myself.

I too, had made progress with managing myself; I hadn't flipped Lola on her back karate-style as my first impulse had been to do. "I accept your apology. I'm glad you're doing better and are out of jail."

"Merry Christmas," Lola said. "Thanks Kat."

She and her sponsor Betty, with Aunt Fae trailing them, headed up onto the porch in the direction of the refreshment table. Pearl was minding the food there from her fancy stand-up wheelchair, with a new prospect member beside her.

I turned with a sigh of relief to face Edith, who gave me a grateful look. "Thank you for letting Lola hug you," she said. "I know how hard that must've been."

"Lola is not the only one who's doing some personal growth," I said. "Let me show you how far I've come." I embraced Edith. I was so much taller than the little lawyer that her pointed hat could fit under my chin.

Josie, Edith's partner, applauded. The Hawaiian woman looked beautiful in a long, royal purple satin muumuu trimmed with rows of crystals, her long hair done in a coronet of braids that supported a red-dyed palm frond hat dressed up with tiny twinkling lights. She tugged her oxygen tank a bit closer and adjusted her cannula before giving me a quick hug. "We sure appreciate you, Kat, and all you've done for Ohia."

"No prob." I flapped a hand dismissively. "Now if only I could find Tiki and Lady Sapphire, Elvira Scarborough's cat, the holiday would be perfect." I told the ladies about my new case as we headed for the refreshments.

"We've seen the flyers around town," Josie said with a slight wheeze as she maneuvered her tank up the steps. "I'm so sorry to hear Tiki is gone, too."

I forced a smile. "Tiki's a survivor. I'm sure she'll turn up. Lady Sapphire, on the other hand, is almost due to have valuable kittens. Someone probably stole her to get at them."

"What's that about a sapphire?" Pearl cupped an ear around her hearing aid. Her sweet little jewel box of a geisha-style headdress swayed with scarlet beads that sparkled like rubies, and the high-necked violet gown she wore proclaimed her timeless style.

"Just my latest case." I raised my voice so she could hear. "Looking for a missing cat."

Pearl nodded. "Come on over and meet my friend Rita Farnsworth. She's checking out the Red Hats, so be on your best behavior."

"That means we'll be cracking some off-color jokes for sure," Edith said, advancing to shake Rita's hand. "I've met you before in Hana. At the chair yoga class at the senior center. You're the teacher."

"Yes," Rita said. "I teach yoga to keep healthy and moving

around and help others do so as well." Rita seemed to be all one color: shoulder-length taupe hair, softly wrinkled beige skin, and oatmeal-colored, baggy flax garments worn over Birkenstocks. "Pearl neglected to tell me the dress code for this event." She reached down to the chair beside her. She lifted a red felt cowboy hat up and put it on. "But at least I have the right topper for the occasion." The ladies clapped and cheered as Rita smiled and made a bow. "I feel right at home."

"All right, everybody. Let's get this party started." Pearl cranked the volume on the boom box, and fast-paced holiday music tinkled even louder. She pointed to the two big punch bowls. "Alcoholic, or virgin? Step right up and pick your poison."

Everyone but Lola and her sponsor opted for the alcoholic.

I had been keeping an eye out for missing group member Clara, curious about who she would bring to the gathering and what she would wear—her trademark looks were striking flowing gowns she sewed herself.

That mystery was solved when Clara drove up and got out of her car in a swirling purple silk muumuu worn with a red satin turban that set off her gleaming, coffee-toned skin.

My eyes further widened at the sight of Dr. Jill Hanson from The Cat Shelter getting out of Clara's car's passenger seat. The retired vet was resplendent in a red satin bolero hat trimmed with swaying purple bobbles. The rest of her outfit was much like mine: a purple sweatshirt with the Shelter's kitten heart logo on it, and a pair of jeans.

Dr. Hanson only wore the hat for a few moments, clearly preferring to show off her brightly dyed, plumage-like hair. Clara and her Red Hat prospect joined the other ladies on the porch, greeting them warmly.

I walked over to the pair with an extra cup of punch in hand. I held it out to the new arrival. "What a treat to see you here, Dr. Hanson! Isn't it a long drive from Kula to an event like this?"

"Please, call me Jill. I don't mind the drive at all. As you know, it's beautiful around the backside of Maui. All that open space, sea, and sky," she smiled.

"Nobody's arguing with that," I agreed.

Clara, her high cheekbones sparkling with glitter, smiled. "It's even more fun when we get to make it into a sleepover weekend with old friends," she said. "Jill needs to get away from her responsibilities more often."

"More like you pried me out of my den of cats," Jill said, laughing. "Fortunately, I have great volunteers who are keeping an eye on The Cat Shelter for me."

"Did you come across any animals this week like the ones we're looking for?" I asked.

"No." Jill shook her head regretfully. "And I've been asking around, too. We did get some new felines in, but they were from the Kahului area."

"Dr. Hanson!" Rita, the new Red Hat prospect, hurried across the porch to embrace Jill enthusiastically. "It's so great to see you. How did you get some time away from your beloved cats?"

"Like I was telling the girls here, I have great volunteers," Jill said. "How is that special project on your property coming along?"

My ears grew an inch, and flipped forward like a bat's as I went on alert, leaning forward to hear more. Sure, 'the special project' could be anything, but I had a feeling it had to do with cats, and these two Cat People knew each other.

Maybe there was a connection to my case. I had to find out more.

15

Almost as if she read my mind, Rita darted a glance around and tugged The Cat Shelter founder by the arm. "Come over to a quiet corner and I'll tell you about it." She drew the retired vet off to the side and leaned in close.

I couldn't read her lips, a skill I had been working on in my Secret Service days but never perfected. "Gosh darn it," I muttered.

Clara waved a hand in front of my face to get my attention. "What's got you so interested?"

"Oh, sorry. I was distracted. Was lost in thought," I said quickly. "K & K Investigations's first case isn't going so well."

"Oh?"

"We're looking for missing cats in this area, specifically a beautiful pedigreed Himalayan who's about to have kittens any day. Her owner is distraught at her loss."

I had been to visit Mrs. Scarborough just a few days ago to report on our lack of progress. I'd needed the packet of tissues I'd thought ahead to bring; the poor woman was a wreck, and her grief had made me miss Tiki even more.

"Yes, I've seen the flyers around town," Clara said. "K & K Investigations? That's you? And who else?"

"The name stands for Kat and Keone," I said, feeling a blush prickle my cheeks. "K & K. It was his idea, I swear."

"I am so happy that you two are moving forward as a couple."

"Well, he has many positive attributes," I said primly.

Clara laughed, her teeth gleaming white. "I'll bet."

The party continued, and though I tried to drift close enough to eavesdrop on Rita and Jill, I had no luck.

I eventually let it go, enjoying the carol singing, delicious food, and potent drinks.

I didn't have to spy on them, because I had made up my mind: I was going to check out Rita's house and see if I could find whatever mysterious project she was working on there.

SUNDAY MORNING I woke with a bit of a hangover from the Red Hat party, and judging from the groans coming from Auntie's room, she had one too. Tiki's absence was an ongoing wound as I patted the empty space beside me on the bed.

Hangover or not, I was determined to follow up with my idea about a surveillance visit to Rita's house. I grabbed my phone from the charger and texted Keone that I had a lead, and did he want to meet me in Hana town?

He replied that he was already gone for the day; he had to fill in for another pilot who was sick and fly a couple of runs into Kahului.

That left me with a wide-open day to work on the case, and post-party blues to shake off.

I threw the covers off and got up to chug water, take a few aspirin, and don my exercise clothes. I planned to go to Hana and find Rita's house, and along the way, I'd blow the hangover out of my system.

Aunt Fae and I both felt better after a second cup of coffee. I retrieved the e-bike from the garage as she put trash bags into the golf cart's rear area to make the rounds of the park, emptying the trashcans from yesterday into a big, locked bin. We worked off our rent at the former model home by providing caretaking services for the park, especially on the weekends when the regular county employees were off. I couldn't have kept up with all of it without Auntie's help.

"See you later for gingerbread house making," I told her. "We'll both be ready for more sugar by then."

"Hard to imagine after yesterday's party binge," Auntie said. "But I've got everything on hand, including candy and royal icing to plaster all over our house. Is Keone coming over?"

"Last I heard," I told her. "He's never made a real gingerbread house before. Said he wouldn't miss it. He has flights today, though, so it'll be after dinner."

"Perfect."

We each hopped onto our respective vehicles and went our separate ways.

I set the coordinates to Rita Farnsworth's address into my phone and pedaled along the road, glad it was early enough for the tourists not to be out yet. I whizzed along twice as fast as a normal bike would go, dodging the reaching branches of a red-blossomed hibiscus and a toad sitting on the road.

What would Rita's house be like?

And what was this secret project of hers?

Time was running out as Lady Sapphire's due date approached.

And what about Tiki? Where could she be?

I glided by Rita's cottage. Her place was on the edge of Hana town at the end of a long driveway. I scanned around, looking for cover and a way to sneak up, but from the general layout, that was going to be difficult.

The front yard was neatly mowed and the asphalt driveway leading to the house and garage was lined with red hibiscus bushes. Rita's bright yellow electric car was pulled into an open shelter beside the main dwelling, an A-frame style home that looked like it had been built in the 1970s. A tall hedge of the same hibiscus bushes that lined the drive surrounded the house's backyard, screening whatever was inside from view.

"Dang it."

I cruised by the property a second time.

The only opportunity to approach undetected had to be from behind the house and grounds. I could conceal the bike and approach from behind the backyard, which butted up against an open, fenced pastoral area.

A few blocks away, I found a grove of java plum trees and parked the bike among them. Once I shed the bright neon Ugliest Helmet and Vest, I was ready for action. I'd dressed for infiltration in a green tee and camouflage running tights with a pair of pull-on, waterproof ankle boots; those would come in handy if I encountered mud and rough terrain.

It still felt a little weird not to be carrying my weapon, but two days before Christmas, in a peaceful town like Hana, and on a mission like searching for a missing cat—well, wearing a gun seemed like overkill.

So to speak.

In lieu of my trusty Glock, I'd loaded my shoulder holster with a can of pepper spray.

After locking up the bike in the brush beneath the trees, I worked my way to the edge of the java plum grove and pushed down three rows of barbed wire atop the cattle fence with a heavy branch. I was tall enough, standing on a stump on one side, to hop over unscathed, landing gracelessly in the tussocky meadow.

I surveyed the pasture; fortunately it looked uninhabited. The grass was long and damp from winter rains. I waded through it, watching for the hibiscus hedge.

That barrier wasn't far. Fortunately, the back of the property hadn't been planted in the thick, impenetrable-looking hedge, but instead was the same fencing as I'd climbed over successfully. Rita probably valued her view out the rear of the property of the green-robed hills in the distance across the pasture.

I sneaked along the edge of the fence, glad of the rubber boots as I stepped squarely in a wet cow patty. "Ugh."

I couldn't worry about the manure clinging to my boot until the mission was accomplished; I was likely to encounter more before this adventure was over.

Finally at the hibiscus hedge, I peered around the tall green barrier with its bright red flowers. My eyes widened at the sight before me.

A massive cage, much like the one I'd seen at The Cat Shelter, filled most of the backyard. Inside, an umbrellalike rain central shelter made of clear ridged roofing covered an elaborate climbing and resting structure covered in indoor-outdoor carpeting.

Cats rested on every visible part of the structure: big ones, little ones. Long and shorthairs. Tabbies, calicos, tuxedos, whites, and seal points. Cats the color of fog and rain, earth, and sunsets. Everywhere the eye could see, cats and more cats.

My heart lifted with a great surge of relief.

This had to be where Lady Sapphire and Tiki were! Adrenaline pumped through me as I looked for a way over the fence.

And then I stopped, frozen in my size elevens, at what I saw next.

16

VISIBLE BEHIND A PART of the carpeted structure, seated in a rocking chair, the sun gleaming on her beige-blonde hair, sat Rita.

A large striped cat occupied her apron-clad lap, and a kitten that she was bottle-feeding rested in her arms. She crooned a lullaby to the baby, tiny enough to fit in the palm of a hand.

Rita Farnsworth appeared to be a cat-loving madonna on her rocker. She was surrounded by onlooking felines who sat around her in an adoring circle.

I wrenched my attention away and surveilled the whole cage, top to bottom, left to right, scanning for my targets.

Against one wall, a constantly flowing fountain provided a water source for several cats to drink, and an enormous self-serve food dispenser kept a feeding trough full for others.

I kept searching for Tiki—but no raccoon size calico missing an ear was visible. That didn't mean she wasn't there, though, sleeping in one of the cozy cubbyholes all over the structure, many of which I couldn't see into.

Next, I scanned for my client's missing pet.

My gaze was soon arrested by a gorgeous longhaired Himalayan, draped sleeping over the tip-top of one of the carpeted cubbies. Lady Sapphire, at last! Relief loosened my locked muscles and my knees sagged. "Thank goodness."

I retreated further behind the hibiscus hedge to consider my next move, but nothing came to me. It was such a lovely scene that I actually hated to disturb Rita. I was stumped.

I could confront Rita, but other than reclaiming the cats I was looking for, had she done anything wrong in rounding up loose animals and caring for them?

And if she refused to let me claim Lady and Tiki, what could I do next?

I peeked at the woman in the rocking chair.

Rita's cheeks gleamed with moisture; *she was crying!*

This woman had suffered some tragedy. There was no doubt. The way Rita held the kitten spoke of profound grief and loss.

She rocked the kitten, singing so softly I couldn't make out the words. I counted two other kittens, nestled in her lap beside the mature cat.

Something was very wrong, and yet very right, about the scene before me.

The layers of content, well-fed animals around Rita seemed to be trying to comfort and absorb her pain. The whole vignette vibrated with pathos.

Before I realized I was chickening out, I found myself halfway back to the java plum grove.

I didn't want to be the one to make things worse for that poor woman. Whose job would that be? The Humane Society? The police? A mental health crisis team?

I needed advice. There was only one person I knew who would have the answers I needed.

Sergeant Detective Leilani Texeira, my friend in the Maui Police Department, picked up right away when I called her cell phone from my perch atop the e-bike. I'd parked at the center of town near Hana's cell phone tower.

"Merry almost Christmas, Kat!" Lei exclaimed cheerfully. I heard toddler Rosie's piping voice in the background, along with the deep barking of the family's big Rottweiler, Conan.

"I hate to disturb you on the weekend," I said. "But I need some professional advice."

"Sure. Let me get out of the chaos so we can talk." I heard the sounds dim and the shutting of a door. "I'm in the back office. Where you spent the night when you and Sophie stayed over, remember? My computer's on already. What do you need?"

There was nothing better than having a friend in law enforcement on speed dial! A surge of gratitude for the amazing women friends I'd made since I moved to Ohia filled my heart. "It's the case Keone and I have been working. It's come to a head and I'm not sure how to proceed."

I told Lei the broad brushstrokes of the job and what I'd discovered at Rita Farnsworth's house. "And in addition, my own cat Tiki has been missing for a similar amount of time."

"Wow. That's a lot to take in," Lei said. "First things first, we need to ascertain if Rita is breaking any local laws. I'm not aware of any specific legislation against housing stray cats, but there might be some zoning regulations or animal welfare laws in play. I'll look into it."

"That would be great, Lei. I appreciate it. Also, there's the issue of reclaiming the missing cats. Lady Sapphire is definitely there, and Tiki could be too," I said.

"Understood. In the case of missing pets, it's a civil matter, not criminal. You'd need the pet owners to confront Rita and demand their pets be returned or take it to small claims court if she refuses. However, given the situation, it might be better to approach this delicately. Rita seems to be dealing with some emotional distress."

"That's what I was thinking, too. I don't want to cause her any more pain, but at the same time, I need to get Tiki, and Lady home to her owner."

"Tread lightly, Kat. We don't want to escalate the matter; it could even turn into a pet hostage situation."

"Oh, ugh! A hostage situation would be terrible!" I exclaimed. "But I can't imagine Rita harming the cats. She seemed so gentle with them. More vulnerable than anything."

"I'll start looking into this from my end and let you know what I find about the legalities. In the meantime, maybe you could try talking to Rita? She might be more cooperative than you think."

"I'll give it a shot, Lei. Thanks for the advice. I'll let you know how it goes."

"Good luck, Kat. And *Mele Kalikimaka*."

"Merry Christmas to you and your family, too." I ended the call and stowed my phone in my pocket. Bracing myself and crossing my fingers for luck, I turned the e-bike to go to Rita's house.

The sun was casting afternoon shadows that danced across the landscape and a breeze had risen, shushing in the coconut palms along the peaceful road. The waning of the day mirrored my own mixed feelings of apprehension and resolve.

As I neared Rita's property, I parked my bike at a distance, careful not to alert her with the sound. Reaching the side of her yard, I walked down the driveway and discovered a small gate beside the house hidden behind an overgrowth of the hibiscus bushes.

I gently unlatched it and prepared to slip into the backyard. The hibiscus hedge was to my right, its flowers a vibrant contrast to the green foliage.

I paused, collecting my thoughts, and calming my racing heart.

I had been at this location before, hidden and observing. Now, I was stepping into the open for a confrontation.

17

I MOVED AWAY from the hedge, entering Rita's backyard.

The woman was still seated in her rocking chair, encircled by the host of cats. All three tiny kittens slept on their backs cradled in her arms, their fuzzy tummies round with milk.

She looked up, startled. Her eyes widened as I approached to stand just outside the enclosure. Her pale brows rose. "I met you at the Red Hat party, but I can't remember your name. What are you doing here?"

"Hello, Rita." I kept my voice steady. "My name is Kat Smith. I need to talk to you about two cats named Lady Sapphire and Tiki."

Rita gently set the kittens into a small basket at her feet. She stood up and dislodged the large tabby from her aproned lap, brushing away stray hairs with her hands. Her face was unreadable as she responded at last, "I don't know any cats by those names. All my cats are strays."

I remained undeterred. "Rita," I said, "I saw Lady Sapphire here earlier." I turned to point at where I'd seen the cat, but the Himalayan was no longer visible. "Her owner is worried about her. And Tiki is my cat. Not a stray. There might be others who you thought were feral, but have owners. We've heard of indoor-outdoor cats missing in this area."

Rita gazed at the animals surrounding her. Her expression filled with sadness, her shoulders drooping. "These cats are all I have," she whispered. "My daughter died years ago of cancer. The holidays are so hard when you're alone." Her words tugged at my heart. The loneliness in her voice was palpable, and I felt a wave of sympathy.

"I'm so sorry for your loss." I took another step closer to the structure.

"These cats are feral. Strays. Unwanted. No one looked for them before."

"Rita," I said gently, "I understand you love these animals. But Lady Sapphire and Tiki have families, and people who miss them. They need to be returned to their true homes. There may be others, too."

Rita sighed deeply, a sound that seemed to resonate around the cat-filled enclosure. "I truly don't know which ones you're talking about," she insisted. "They're all special to me."

"I can identify them, Rita," I said with resolute calmness. "Let me come inside and look for them."

Rita's expression was a mix of defiance and sorrow as she crossed her arms on her chest, gazing around at the cats. Interestingly, the animals showed little interest in me, unlike those at The Cat Shelter. Their attention remained on Rita. Finally Rita's gaze met mine, a myriad of emotions flickering in her blue eyes. "I didn't . . . I didn't mean to take anyone's pet. I thought they were lost. Lonely," she confessed in a hushed tone. "Like me."

"I understand," I said. "But we need to do what's right. For Lady Sapphire, for Tiki, and perhaps for others here as well."

Rita looked down and her hands nervously wrung the edge of her apron. "I . . . I don't know which ones they are."

"May I?" I asked, indicating the motley collection of cats surrounding her. At her nod, I stepped forward, opening the simple latch door and walking forward to scrutinize each feline and cubbyhole in search of Tiki and Lady Sapphire.

After a thorough search, my chest tightened with disappointment. The beautiful Himalayan turned out to be a spayed male, and none of the cubbies contained my familiar kink-tailed, one-eared calico.

Neither of our targets was there.

I turned to address Rita, disappointment making my shoulders sag.

"Neither Tiki nor Lady Sapphire is here," I said, my voice low.

Rita frowned. "That's too bad."

"It's okay," I said, though my chest felt heavy as lead. "We'll find them. But we need to make sure this doesn't happen again. Missing pets, who end up in your cage."

Rita nodded. "I . . . I just wanted to help the endangered birds," she murmured. "And the cats. There are so many feral ones all over the island."

"How did you capture all of these?" I gestured to the felines shedding hair all over my pants as they wound around my legs.

"I had the help of two kind young men, Chad and Dave."

My eyebrows shot up. "Chad? Our mail deliverer?"

"Yes. Chad set traps in Kahului and brought those he captured out here. He would also empty the ones Dave set up around town, then drop all the cats he caught here at my house. He hid them in the back of the mail truck."

I remembered the wall of boxes at the rear of the truck that never seemed to move. He must have had his captives behind it.

"Hmm," I said. "No wonder Chad was looking so tired before the holidays with all that extra work. It's abuse of postal property to use the truck that way and double dip on his salary."

"Please don't get him fired, Kat." Rita made prayer hands. "Chad's a sweet young man who wanted to help with the problem and earn a little extra money that I was happy to pay him. Dave, too. He's the one who got his friend Chad involved. He built this big cat house for me."

Now I knew what Dave had been doing with the rolls of chicken wire!

"Okay." I would have to talk to my boss, Mr. Hanoi, about Chad, but I didn't need to tell Rita that. "Please stop collecting more cats until we figure out what the legalities are for this situation, okay?"

"I understand."

"You can help the genuine strays as long as it's not against the law, and I don't think it is though I have a detective looking into it for us. But first, we need to make sure any cat you currently have is really without a home. Maybe we could check for microchips or find out if they're being searched for."

After a moment, Rita nodded. "Yes," she agreed. "That sounds like a good plan. I hope you find the pets you're looking for."

"Me too. I'll be in touch."

I left Rita's yard and headed for my bike.

Tiki and Lady Sapphire were still gone, but at least I knew what was going on with all the missing cats and who'd trapped them. We'd still have something to celebrate tonight when Keone came over and we made gingerbread houses with Aunt Fae.

18

I RODE HOME AND, when I got there, updated Lei with the outcome of my talk with Rita. Lei notified the Humane Society about Rita's cats and told me they would send an animal control team with a portable chip reader out to Rita's house tomorrow, Christmas Eve. They would check for missing pets among the strays in the enclosure and make sure everything met all county requirements.

Still feeling bad that I hadn't found Lady Sapphire, I called Elvira Scarborough. I told her that I'd found a lot of cats, but not hers. With Aunt Fae's blessing, I invited her to join us for an evening of gingerbread decorating. "Wouldn't you like to get out of your house and do something festive?"

Mrs. Scarborough agreed to come and was due to arrive at the same time as Keone.

I took a shower, blow-dried my long hair, and swiped on mascara and lipstick. I dressed in black pants paired with my "ugly" Christmas sweater—a favorite Aunt Fae had produced from one of her many packages from Maine. The woven cotton number featured a grinning reindeer face with big antlers. HORNY was spelled out below the reindeer head. I grinned at the thought of Keone's expression when he saw it.

That cheered me up a bit, along with the homely scent of gingerbread wafting up the stairs from Aunt Fae's kitchen. The comforting aroma provided contrast to the worry gnawing at my gut.

Where the heck were Lady and Tiki?

But I'd done all I could for the moment. The holiday was upon us, and it was time to be festive. I heard the doorbell chiming at the front door as I finished my grooming, and I flew down the stairs.

"I'll get it!" I hollered to Aunt Fae in the kitchen. I flung the door open with a wide smile and a welcoming gesture. "Happy holidays!"

Keone and Mrs. Scarborough stood on the top step. They had been conversing, and now they turned to me. Their jaws dropped simultaneously at the sight of my sweater.

Mrs. Scarborough colored up and covered her mouth with a hand, giggling. "My goodness, dear, that is . . ."

"The best ugly sweater I've ever seen," Keone finished. He stepped across the threshold to take me in his arms. "I love it."

He kissed me, and that went on for a bit which required Aunt Fae to usher Mrs. Scarborough in and offer her refreshments.

Now my client sat across from me at the dining room table, piping icing onto her gingerbread construction. Instrumental carols played in the background, drifting from the speaker I'd let Aunt Fae open early for the occasion.

"It's good to be here," Mrs. Scarborough said, a smile lifting her wan features. "Thank you for inviting me."

"Of course, Mrs. Scarborough. I'm just sorry we didn't find Lady for you."

"Please, call me Elvira. And I know you tried your best."

I shook my head in regret. "Elvira, I was so sure Lady would be in that cage I found. We so wanted to get her home for you before her kittens were due."

"Wherever Lady is, I just pray that she's being well-cared-for."

"And I hope the same thing for my missing cat, Tiki."

As I tried to concentrate on assembling my gingerbread house, Keone and Aunt Fae, in the kitchen, engaged in a playful competition of decorating sugar cookies for the roof. Their laughter echoed into the dining room along with the sound of the festive music.

"Kat," Elvira noted with a soft chuckle, "the roof of your gingerbread house is upside-down."

I glanced down at my gingerbread construction, realizing my error. "I guess I'm a bit distracted," I admitted, flipping the roof to the correct orientation.

Keone placed a warm hand on my shoulder. "Still concerned about Rita and those cats?" he asked.

"And where Tiki and Lady are," I said.

The sudden buzz of Keone's cell phone interrupted our conversation. He glanced at the screen, his brows furrowing slightly. "It's the Nakasone family landline," he said, and answered the call with a quizzical expression. "Hey there. What's up?"

The family must have his number from when he dated her Aunt Lani before I arrived in Ohia. My eyebrows rose as he addressed Sandy, who had made the call. What was a nine-year-old calling Keone for?

The serious expression on Keone's face as he listened to her sent a wave of alarm through me.

"I'll be right there," he said, and ended the call. He glanced at Aunt Fae, Elvira, and me. "We have to go help the girls right now. It's an emergency."

19

"LADY SAPPHIRE IS at the Nakasone girls' house," Keone said, his voice concerned. "And the poor cat is sick. The girls are home alone and don't know what to do."

"Oh no! Lady must be having her kittens!" Elvira exclaimed, jumping to her feet. "I'll call the mobile vet. I have him on speed dial already." The older woman fumbled her phone out of the pocket of her loose pants.

"Elvira, tell the vet to meet us at the Nakasones' house," Keone instructed, and told her the address on Plumeria Street.

"Let's worry about how Lady came to be at the girls' house later," I said. Elvira nodded, already preoccupied with making the call.

Meanwhile, Aunt Fae jumped into action. "We'll need to gather some supplies for the birth—towels, a first-aid kit, soft cat chow, and a carrier," she said, moving briskly around the kitchen. "Plus, food for all involved."

Everything kicked into high gear. Elvira spoke to the vet, her voice jittering with a mix of haste and excitement. Meanwhile, Keone and I turned into Aunt Fae's personal assistants, scrambling around to gather the supplies she directed us to.

Aunt Fae somehow managed to fit everything into a single tote bag topped by the cat carrier. My arms sagged under its weight as she handed it to me. The gravity of our mission had decided to manifest itself in a very literal sense.

Soon we were ready to go. Keone led the way to Sharkey and Elvira got into her own car parked beside it in the driveway.

The air was thick with the scent of the recent rain, and the lush greenery of the area seemed to be watching us in silent anticipation. We made it to the Nakasone home in record time with Keone at the wheel of the white SUV.

Sandy and her sister were waiting for us with the front door ajar, their faces stricken and pinched. "Thanks for coming, Uncle Keone," Sandy said in a subdued voice. "We didn't know who to call."

Windy narrowed her eyes at me but remained silent as we trooped up onto the porch. I had plenty of questions for the girls, starting with how the heck they had Lady in the first place—but decided to save them for later, as both girls looked chastened and tear-stained, worry for the cat clear in their postures.

They led us to Lady Sapphire, who was nestled in a blanket on the living room couch. The Himalayan cat looked enormous, her sides distended with pregnancy. She gave a wavering, miserable mew at the sight of us.

My heart went out to her. Who knew a cat could stir up such emotions?

Elvira Scarborough flew across the room to kneel beside her pet. "Oh, sweetie. I'm here now, and so glad to see you."

The unhappy meow turned to a purr as Lady rubbed her head on Elvira's hand.

I glanced at the Nakasone girls. However they'd come to have Lady, they had to have seen the posters around town and known she wasn't a stray. The two had turned to each other and were crying silently in each other's arms.

Aunt Fae and I began the construction of what I decided to call

'Fort Sapphire,' using the towels and carrier. "She will likely be more comfortable in a cavelike, cozy setting," Auntie said.

Meanwhile, Keone spoke to the girls. "Lady's not sick. She's having kittens and the vet is on his way. Lady Sapphire is in good hands."

"Or she will be, soon," I said. "And meantime, we'll take care of her as well as a bunch of amateur cat midwives can."

Sandy and Windy came to sit on either side of Lady as Elvira knelt in front of the Himalayan. "We found her on the street in Hana," Sandy said.

"We didn't know she had an owner," Windy said. "She didn't have a collar."

I bit my lips on a rebuttal—how could that be true? Lady was kept securely in her backyard. Someone had to have taken her out on purpose.

Elvira Scarborough's gaze took in the girls' unkempt appearance and the house's humble furnishings. "As long as Lady's okay, I don't care how she came to be here," she said. "I can see you took good care of her, and I'm glad you called for help when she needed it."

The vet arrived, his professional demeanor immediately putting us at ease. Relief washed over us as he set to work, examining Lady Sapphire, and preparing for the imminent arrival of her kittens.

As we watched the vet in action, a mix of worry and hope filled the room.

Despite the circumstances, there was a sense of unity among us —a shared determination to see this through together. In that moment, I couldn't help but appreciate Keone, Aunt Fae, the vet, Sandy and Windy, and Elvira most of all. Her gracious attitude regarding the girls had created an atmosphere where everyone could calm down and bond.

Lady Sapphire seemed to benefit most of all. Surrounded by love and support, the cat visibly relaxed between contractions, purring, and flexing her paws as Elvira stroked and cooed to her. "She'll be a mother any moment now," the vet said.

I could hardly wait to see the kittens. I reached out and took Keone's hand and squeezed it hard, my eyes prickling, as Lady's first baby entered the world.

The first kitten born was a petite little thing, her coat as gray and white as the snow-capped Himalayas. The second, a bit larger, sported a distinct dark smudge on its forehead. Keone remarked, "That's not a birthmark, that's a badge of honor for surviving!" This earned a few smiles around the room.

Just when we thought Lady Sapphire was done with her labors, the vet announced, "Looks like we've got a bonus."

A third kitten made its entrance, the smallest of the lot but with a loud mew that drowned out the others, causing Lady to turn and give it extra attention. "That one's the squeaky wheel," Aunt Fae observed.

Once Lady Sapphire and her kittens were declared healthy and well, the vet took his leave amid many thanks and holiday wishes.

Elvira approached me, her eyes shining with joy. "Looks like we've got a trio of champions here," she said, her voice filled with warmth and happiness. "It's going to be so wonderful watching them grow. They're already spoken for by future owners, you know."

She let the girls touch the kittens as they nursed, and stroke Lady's head as the new mother lay purring softly, her eyes half shut with tiredness and contentment.

Eventually it was time for Elvira to leave with Lady Sapphire and her newborns. We helped her pack up 'Fort Sapphire,' ensuring the little feline family would be comfortable for their ride home.

As Elvira left, she turned to say, "Thank you, girls, for calling for help when Lady needed it, and for taking such good care of her."

The girls nodded, clearly guilt-stricken, but remained quiet as Elvira left with the carrier, closing the door behind her.

With Elvira gone, the house immediately felt empty in spite of the five of us crowded into the small living room.

Aunt Fae tried to turn the mood around. "Well, I think we have some unfinished business," she said, her eyes twinkling. "We left in the middle of a big project we could use some help with." She turned to the Nakasone girls. "How about you two come over to our house, and we finish decorating several gingerbread houses?"

The girls' faces lit up at the suggestion. They called their father for permission on the landline, and then we all piled into Sharkey for the short drive to our house.

The five of us spent the rest of the evening in a whirlwind of frosting, candies, and edible glitter. The gingerbread houses turned out to be more sugar than structure, but the laughter and camaraderie made up for their architectural shortcomings.

As I looked around the house, now filled with the sweet smell of gingerbread and the memory of a joyous evening, it was hard not to marvel at how the day had unfolded. Sitting on the couch, nibbling a sugar roof tile and sipping hot apple cider, I watched Keone helping Windy pipe the edge of her house as Aunt Fae washed up some dishes. Sandy came and sat beside me on the couch.

"You had to have known everyone was looking for Lady Sapphire," I said gently.

Sandy looked down at her hands. She licked a bit of frosting off one of her fingers.

"Windy brought the cat home after going to play at a friend's house in Hana. She said she found her lost in the street. She didn't have a collar on. Windy called her Princess." Sandy glanced up at me with troubled brown eyes. "I knew Windy was lying, especially after I saw the poster in the post office. But Princess made her so happy. I couldn't tell on her. We kept Princess inside our rooms and hid her when Dad and Auntie came home. They never noticed we kept the doors shut when they were there. Princess slept a lot. Now I know why—she was getting ready to have her babies." Sandy's eyes filled and overflowed. "She is such a pretty, sweet cat. We're going to miss her so much."

"You took good care of her," I said. "You knew when to call for help when she was in distress. The vet said she was well-nourished, and her coat looked beautiful."

"I brushed her every day." Windy must have been listening in because she continued, "Maybe Mrs. Scarborough will let us have one of her kittens." Her eyes shone with hope.

"The kittens are very valuable," I said gently. "She said they are all spoken for."

Windy's head fell forward like a flower on a wilted stem. "I don't know why I said that. She would never give us a kitten. We're lucky she didn't call the cops on us."

Keone and I exchanged a helpless glance; Windy was right about that. He patted the little girl's back. "Maybe your dad will let you get a different cat."

Aunt Fae cleared her throat from the kitchen. "Have you girls seen the movie, *It's a Wonderful Life?*"

They shook their heads.

"Well, you'll love it. We should eat one of these gingerbread houses and watch it together. Give me your dad's phone number and I'll call and ask if you can stay later and get picked up after it's over."

The girls brightened a bit at this. Both of them squeezed in on one side next to me on the couch. "Do you have popcorn, Auntie?" Sandy asked. "Popcorn makes movies better, our mom used to say."

"Sure do, sweetheart," Auntie said, fetching some microwave popcorn from the cupboard.

Keone joined us, sitting on the other side of me. After the popcorn was ready, Aunt Fae handed the bag to the girls. We settled in, munching popcorn and gingerbread washed down with apple cider, and enjoyed the movie.

Aunt Fae to the rescue, once again.

20

CHRISTMAS EVE, the following day, fell on a Monday. Our remote post office location was only open half a day. I put on a Santa hat and Pua wore a green elf cap trimmed in golden bells. We exchanged gifts before opening up: she'd bought me a set of refill cartridges for the vapor scent diffuser in my office, and I'd bought her a delicate pair of crystal snowflake earrings that she promptly put on. "They look perfect with your elf outfit," I told her.

She laughed. "That's not a sentence you hear every day."

"Maybe only on Christmas Eve!"

We'd come a long way from the early, difficult days when I first arrived in Ohia.

I wrote FOUND on all the posters around our area advertising Lady Sapphire's loss, and reported her discovery to our customers as they came in.

Chad arrived with the day's mail and a hangdog look and apology to me. He told us he was not yet fired, though he'd been written up and was on probation for his role in the Great Cat Snatch Caper. Our boss, Mr. Hanoi, had taken him to task about use of the postal service vehicle for nonwork activities. "I promise

I'll never do it again," he told us earnestly. "I knew it was wrong to use the truck, but I thought I was helping the cats. Really."

"And maybe you were," I said. "Happy holidays, cat burglar."

He snorted a laugh, and I gave him a plate of Aunt Fae's cookies which he gratefully accepted before getting on the road.

The short hours of the day flew by, filled with all the last-minute packages and cards to be sorted and picked up.

Meanwhile, Lei called me and told me that the Humane Society went out to Rita Farnsworth's with the chip reader. The Red Hats went too and gathered around Rita to sponsor and present a proposal that her house become an extension site of The Cat Shelter. Rita decided to partner with Dr. Jill Hanson, officially, and everyone seemed to feel good about that as Dr. Hanson agreed to cover and supervise Rita's feline care efforts through her nonprofit.

The Humane Society staffers checked all the cats Rita had on site. They removed four with microchips and took them home to their owners—a perfect Christmas Eve gift.

They then allowed Rita to keep all the animals she'd collected "as long as an appropriate level of care is maintained."

Soon it was time for Pua and me to lock up the post office. We exchanged a holiday hug and put a "Closed for the Holiday" sign on the door, bidding each other "Merry Christmas!"

My heart lifted with apprehension/excitement: it was time for Aunt Fae and I to get dressed and go to the Kaihales' legendary holiday luau in Hana. Ilima Kaihale's parties were reputed to be as Hawaiian as the hula dance itself—but would we truly be welcome?

Even with Mr. K texting me ongoing update photos of loading the *imu* and other prep for the gathering, I couldn't help worrying that as 'Maine-iacs' fresh off the plane, we wouldn't fit in.

Aunt Fae and I dressed in our best holiday wear: she in a crisp cotton aloha shirt bedecked with Santas wearing leis paired with jeans, and I in a fitted sheath dress in holiday red that Pua had insisted I buy online. "You've got a great figure, Kat, but you never show it off," she'd said, showing me the dress on her phone. "Christmas is a time to really shine. Don't you want to make Keone's eyes pop when he sees you?"

So I'd upgraded the black dress with a gun pocket that I'd worn to a million state department events in Washington, DC and retired it, in favor of this new scarlet number with a slit that ran up one thigh.

Aunt Fae eyed my outfit from the top of my head to the strappy sandals I wore as I drove Sharkey toward Hana. "You're brighter than a winter cardinal in that dress," she said. "Prettier, too. I love it."

"Thanks, Auntie."

There were so many cars along the shoulders of the road that we had to park a distance away. We approached on foot, carrying our offerings. Ilima's house nestled between swaying palms and vibrant bougainvillea down a driveway lined with gardenia bushes. The tantalizing aroma of the traditional *imu*, an underground oven, enveloped us. The scent was smoky and earthy, carrying the essence of Hawaii itself. Cooked that way, the kalua pig inside promised to be a gustatory experience to remember.

Inside the open, concrete floor garage where the family gathered, tables sagged under the weight of the many delicacies. There was *poi*, the iconic taro root dish, its unique, slightly sour taste a perfect complement to the rich kalua pig that was soon to be unearthed. Plates of *lomi* salmon, a refreshing mix of tomatoes, onions, and salty fish, offered a burst of colors and flavors. And for those with a sweet tooth, there was *haupia*, my favorite, a creamy coconut dessert that was a perfect palate cleanser at the end of a meal.

Despite the tantalizing aromas, lively strumming of ukuleles, happy chatter and many hugs, my heart felt heavy with sadness I hid behind a smile. The luau seemed to lack sparkle, a night sky without its stars, as I yearned for the familiar purr and even the grumpy demands of Tiki, my absent feline friend. She'd loved to hover on the edges of parties, darting in to steal a treat now and again while keeping a watchful eye on my safety.

Keone approached, his eyes widening. He whistled, giving me an appreciative once-over. "You're gorgeous tonight, Kat."

I mustered a smile and let him pull me in for a hug.

"You're not so bad yourself." I slid my hands up and around his neck, petting the rich silk he wore. "You look amazing in this dark purple."

"Mom said so too, that's why she gave me this dress shirt as my holiday gift." His pearly teeth gleamed; he was altogether splendid.

"I approve."

"And you're my lady in red." He put his mouth close to my ear and spoke gently. "Kat, you're not fooling me. You look as glum as a tourist who has to get on a flight home to the mainland. What's up?"

I sighed as I rested my chin on Keone's shoulder. "I'm so glad we found Lady, and that her kittens are happy and healthy. But I'm still missing Tiki. I really thought I'd found her at Rita's . . . but now I'm giving up hope. I've lost her."

Keone nodded, his warm brown eyes reflecting understanding along with the colored sparkle lights strung around the party area. "Tiki's one in a million. Free-spirited as the trade winds. She'll come home when she's ready. Until then . . ." He pointed to a raised wooden stage set up on the lawn with an open tent over it in case of rain showers. A mischievous glint lit his eye. "How about a dance?"

Before I could respond, he gestured to the deejay, a high school kid with a set of tech tools on a folding table. The notes of the *12 Days of Christmas* tune boomed out of speakers around us. I glanced around wildly as the crowd erupted in cheers. My friend Artie came and took a seat beside the teenage deejay, his guitar in hand.

"What's this song? The tune is familiar."

"A new twist on a holiday favorite." Keone, with the enthusiasm of a child opening a present, tugged me onto the crowded "dance floor." The crowd sang along as Artie belted out the song into a mic, accompanied by dramatic strumming chords.

*"**Numbah One** day of Christmas, my tutu give to me*
One mynah bird in one papaya tree.

***Numbah Two** day of Christmas, my tutu give to me*
Two coconut, an' one mynah bird in one papaya tree.

***Numbah Tree** day of Christmas, my tutu give to me*
Tree dry squid, two coconut
An' one mynah bird in one papaya tree.

***Numbah Foah** day of Christmas, my tutu give to me*
Foah flowah lei, tree dry squid, two coconut
An' one mynah bird in one papaya tree.

***Numbah Five** day of Christmas, my tutu give to me*
Five beeg fat peeg, foah flowah lei, tree dry squid, two coconut
An' one mynah bird in one papaya tree.

***Numbah Six** day of Christmas, my tutu give to me*
Six hula lesson, five beeg fat peeg, foah flowah lei, tree dry squid, two coconut
An' one mynah bird in one papaya tree.

***Numbah Seven** day of Christmas, my tutu give to me*
Seven shrimp a-swimmin', six hula lesson, five beeg fat peeg, foah flowah lei, tree dry squid, two coconut
An' one mynah bird in one papaya tree.

***Numbah Eight** day of Christmas, my tutu give to me*
Eight ukulele, seven shrimp a-swimmin', six hula lesson, five beeg fat peeg, foah flowah lei, tree dry squid, two coconut
An' one mynah bird in one papaya tree.

***Numbah Nine** day of Christmas, my tutu give to me*
Nine pound of poi, eight ukulele, seven shrimp a-swimmin', six hula lesson, five beeg fat peeg, foah flowah lei, tree dry squid, two coconut
An' one mynah bird in one papaya tree.

***Numbah Ten** day of Christmas, my tutu give to me*
Ten can of beer, nine pound of poi, eight ukulele, seven shrimp a-

swimmin', six hula lesson, five beeg fat peeg, foah flowah lei, tree dry squid, two coconut

An' one mynah bird in one papaya tree.

Numbah Eleven *day of Christmas, my tutu give to me*

Eleven missionary, ten can of beer, nine pound of poi, eight ukulele, seven shrimp a-swimmin', six hula lesson, five beeg fat peeg, foah flowah lei, tree dry squid, two coconut

An' one mynah bird in one papaya tree.

Numbah Twelve *day of Christmas, my tutu give to me*

Twelve TELEVISION, eleven missionary, ten can of beer, nine pound of poi, eight ukulele, seven shrimp a-swimmin', six hula lesson, five beeg fat peeg, foah flowah lei, tree dry squid, two coconut

An' one mynah bird in one papaya tree!"

As we improvised moves to the music, Keone's actions were hilarious. His rendition of 'four flower leis' involved an exaggerated pantomime of being strangled by the leis, and for 'six hula lessons,' he pranced around, gyrating his hips.

He was so funny that my sadness floated away on laughter.

This guy. How'd I get to be so lucky?

As the song ended and we came to a halt, breathless and grinning, Aunt Fae joined us. Her bright eyes matched a garland of golden stars glinting on her silver hair. "Keone, that hula would have made even Tiki crack up," she said. "And look what's right overhead." She pointed above us, where a sprig of plastic mistletoe tied with red ribbon swayed over the dance area. "I believe you owe him a kiss."

"You're right as usual, Aunt Fae." I swooped Keone into my arms, catching him by surprise. I dipped him low over my thigh, kissing him thoroughly, to the cheers of his rowdy family.

When I pulled him up, red and laughing, his mother Ilima put her fingers in her mouth and emitted a piercing wolf whistle. "When's the wedding?" she yelled, and everyone laughed.

Keone and I ducked our heads and ran for refills at the punch bowl.

As the luau swirled on into the night, the evening filled with joy, music, and the irresistible taste and smell of Hawaiian food. I could feel Tiki's spirit was among us. In our shared camaraderie, she was there, a calico ghost on the fringes.

If I never saw my beloved hellcat again in this life, I was finally able to be grateful for every day we'd had together.

21

CHRISTMAS MORNING in Ohia broke over the island, and I lay in bed looking at the colored lights surrounding the bay window with its view of a green hill lined with palm trees.

Holidays in Hawaii were a unique blend of traditional holiday cheer and tropical charm. It still felt a little strange not to have snow, short days, and heavy weather outside as we did in Maine at this time of year, but as I listened to the sound of cooing doves and distant roosters outside, I decided to make the most of that difference with an early morning swim.

I stayed where I was for a moment in bed, watching as the sky gradually lightened from the deep indigo of night to a vibrant palette of pinks and oranges. The distant palm trees swayed gently in the balmy breeze, their fronds making a sound like rain on leaves.

The rich scent of Kona coffee, freshly brewed, tantalized me, mixing with the nutmeg-laced fragrance of eggnog Auntie had heated on the stove during an early morning baking spree I'd dimly heard, smelled, and slept through. She must be in bed again now, as I didn't hear anything from her room.

I tossed my comforter aside, ignoring the familiar pang of loss at Tiki's absence. I threw on my bathing suit and the rash guard Keone had given me as a warmth layer. I donned a pair of running shorts and my beloved Nikes, then tossed a beach towel around my neck and padded down the stairs.

The house was quietly alive with festive spirit. The smell of cinnamon and vanilla floated around the kitchen, a testament to Aunt Fae's baking. The makeshift Christmas tree Aunt Fae and I had fashioned from local driftwood nailed to a wooden stand stood proudly in the corner of the living room, adorned with glowing lights and handmade shell and coral ornaments plus precious heirloom glass pieces from our history in Maine. The soft strains of a ukulele rendition of '*Mele Kalikimaka*' hummed in the background on Auntie's new speaker, adding a local touch to the holiday atmosphere.

I glanced at Tiki's empty sleeping basket and full food bowl. They were a stark reminder of her loss, and my heart ached.

"Thanks, Auntie. You make everything better," I murmured to the ceiling where my hardworking surrogate mom slumbered. At the counter, I filled a mug with coffee and grabbed a piece of soft, fresh cinnamon swirl bread. Inside the house was wonderful, but as always, I was drawn to the outdoors, seeking solace in the gentle ocean breeze as I let myself outside.

I ate the bread and drank the coffee from my DO NOT SPEAK TO ME UNTIL THIS IS EMPTY mug as I walked briskly down the artfully weaving road through New Ohia Park. As always, I scanned for any sign of Tiki as I made my way past the entry signage and across the street to the deserted early morning beach at Ohia Bay.

Christmas Day meant the Hana Highway was empty for once, and so was the beach. The sun broke over the ocean, casting a warm glow on everything it touched. The scent of the salty sea air mingled with the sweet fragrance of plumeria flowers, creating a tropical bouquet that was distinctly Ohia.

I spread my towel on the sand and sat, watching the ocean for a moment, and practicing gratitude for all my many blessings. A whale blew outside the bay, making my heart lift, and a sandpiper darted in and out among the gentle waves.

Gradually a sense of peace filled me.

Peace, hope, and gratitude were the real reasons for the season, and this morning I felt all three.

I was also especially thankful that I didn't have a hangover from the Kaihales' luau.

I set my phone and mug aside and rose to my feet, shedding my shoes and getting ready to go in for a swim.

Suddenly, in the distance, a loud, demanding meow broke through the rhythmic sound of the waves. I turned in the direction the sound was coming from, my heart pounding—*that was Tiki's familiar cry!*

Could she be calling me, as she had so often in the past?

I looked across the street at the shack where I'd lived for my first months on Ohia.

The impatient, demanding cry came again. As if she been conjured by a genie, Tiki appeared, emerging from under the shack just behind the post office. She sat down imperiously on the beach rock top step, just as she'd done a thousand times before.

She stared over at me, and yowled impatiently as if to say, "Don't you see me? What's wrong with you? I want food now!"

"Tiki!" I yelled in delight. I ran barefoot across the street, and squatted to pet her one-eared head, lightheaded with relief. "Where have you been, you crazy cat? You put me through heck!"

Tiki rose and wound herself around my legs, purring—and that's when I felt how thin she'd become, her belly loose and flappy as an empty sack.

"You were sick. That's what was wrong. You were ill and you were hiding down here," I crooned, stroking her bony back. "Oh, my sweet girl, I'm so glad to see you!"

Tiki gave a commanding "meow!" as if to summon me, and slid out from under my hand to disappear beneath the porch.

"Oh my gosh," I muttered. "What is she up to now?"

I was familiar with the dark, musty crawlspace under the shack. Intimately familiar, in fact. I'd constructed a hideout down there made of recycled boxes that had saved my life from an assassin—a story for another day.

I peered under the porch just in time to see Tiki disappear inside the simple cardboard shelter I'd never bothered to remove.

"What on this green earth is Tiki doing?" I wasn't about to belly crawl across the dirt to see what she was up to in there—I had a much better way to check that out.

I hurried up on the porch and unlocked the front door with keys I was lucky enough to have in my shorts pocket, grabbed a flashlight from the utility drawer, and hurried to the bathroom. I pushed up the wood flap behind a built-in shelf beside the shower.

This was the entry Tiki used to get inside the living area, and it led to my hidey-hole in the crawlspace under our house. I hadn't thought to check the cardboard fort under the shack in my frantic search of our new neighborhood.

I pushed the flap open and peered down into the shadows, shining my flashlight into the crude fort.

A pair of large, familiar yellow eyes blinked up at me—and several smaller pairs stared up at me, too.

Tiki was surrounded by kittens.

"Tiki, you naughty hellcat." These kits weren't newborns; they had their eyes open and were moving around freely on their own. My sneaky pet must have come down to the shack and given birth within the first day of going missing.

"Sweet girl, you're a mama!" I whispered, my voice catching in my throat. Relief and joy washed over me as Tiki let out another commanding mew. "You want me to come down there and meet your babies?"

Tiki had been sitting upright amid the welter of kittens crawling and climbing over and around her; now she started up her motorboat purr as if to confirm her desire for me to join them. She stretched out on the beach towel I'd brought down previously for her as a bed.

The kittens immediately pounced all over her and each other in a multicolored mewing mound; they eventually sorted themselves out and began nursing.

"Oh, my goodness. I count five kittens here, Tiki. No wonder we thought you were getting fat. And no wonder you're so skinny now." I carefully slid into the fort and sat cross-legged beside my cat, stroking her head and blinking away tears. "I never did get you to the vet for a checkup, and now look what happened. You're a mother!"

This discovery was a Christmas miracle I hadn't dared to hope for. The day had started with a palpable absence, and now it was filled with the wholeness and joy of reunion with my beloved missing cat.

22

THE EMOTIONAL REUNION with Tiki and the unexpected
introduction of her kittens needed to be shared with Aunt Fae.
Also, Keone would be arriving soon for our Christmas Day tradition of present opening, gingerbread eating, and reading new
books.

I wouldn't ruin the surprise by texting them about finding Tiki;
showing was more powerful than telling.

Grinning the whole way, I hurried out of the fort and fetched a
cardboard box from the recycle pile behind the post office building.
As I was folding the box into a rectangle shape, Artie and Opal
emerged from the depths of the Ohia General Store to greet the day
on the porch as was their habit.

"*Mele Kalikimaka*, Kat!" Opal hollered across the parking lot.
Today, the velour scarf draping her shoulders was an eye-popping
red and green stripe worn over a muumuu dotted with a candy
cane design. Artie, guitar under his arm, wore a fuzzy, short-sleeved
Santa suit with his rubber slippers.

"Merry Christmas to you as well. You two sure are festive!" I
picked my way around the puddles in the parking lot, wincing as a
stone poked my bare foot. "I have news."

"And where are your shoes?" Opal put her hands on her hips sternly. Artie strummed a dramatic chord.

"I was too excited to get them; they're over at the beach. Tiki reappeared—and you'll never guess what else."

Artie intoned, "dun-dun-dun," accompanied by strums on the guitar.

"Tell us, already!" Opal exclaimed.

I brandished the large box. "She was hiding under the shack this whole time with a litter of kittens. Five of them!"

Opal clapped her hands to her cheeks. "What?"

"I know, right?" I shook my head. "I don't know why it never crossed my mind Tiki wasn't fixed. Maybe because . . ." I cupped a hand around my mouth in an exaggerated whisper, "She's not exactly the maternal type. But it turns out she's a great mom and has raised babies that all look healthy and happy."

"We'll take one. Maybe two," Opal said instantly. "One for each of us."

"Ho-ho-ho!" Artie bellowed in his best Santa imitation. He nodded vigorously, grinning, and making the fuzzy bobble on his red velvet hat bounce. "A kitten each is the perfect Christmas present!"

"Great," I said. "Now I've only got three more to find homes for!" I was already thinking of two little girls who'd be overjoyed to have a kitten apiece.

"We can take them all to get spayed and neutered with their mother," Opal said. "Make sure there aren't any more surprise litters in the neighborhood."

"Definitely. Maybe with her kittens in the carrier, I could get Tiki inside to take her to the vet. I never could before; she was too wild to get into the carrier, let alone the car." I waggled the cardboard box. "I am going to get the kittens out from under the shack and take them home. Want to see them when I do?"

"Wouldn't miss it," Artie said. "I don't need sight to enjoy that."

"I'm so excited!" Opal clasped her hands together, her pale blue eyes shining, her spiky white hair aquiver. "What did I tell you? The runes were right. This is a new beginning, in all kinds of ways." "One hundred percent!" I agreed.

WITH SOME COAXING, Tiki allowed me to put her babies into the box, now lined with the beach towel I'd fetched when I went back and put on my shoes.

Each of the kittens was unique, except for a pair of orange tabbies so identical I couldn't tell them apart. A mist gray with white socks found a spot beside a snowy white kitten with a tail so black it looked like it had been dipped in ink. And last but not least, a tiny calico, the runt of the litter, splotched in brown, black, white, and orange, took her place right in the middle.

I settled the kits in the sturdy box, petting their tiny heads, enjoying their soft warmth and the sweet little mews they emitted as I handled them. Tiki, kinked tail high and eyes bright, trotted beside me as I exited the shack with the box and locked it up.

Opal and Artie came down from the store's porch. Exclaiming over the kittens, they immediately called dibs on the pair of orange tabbies. "They're twins. They should stay together," Opal said. She carefully lifted each of them up and examined them. "And they're both boys."

"Let's call them Tom and Jerry," Artie said. And so it was.

As I carried the box home, relieved to have my shoes on again to protect my feet, the sun, higher now, warmed up the dew-kissed leaves. Palms rustled gently overhead, cardinals chirped, mynahs squawked, and the distant murmur of waves faded as we walked home.

"I never did get that swim," I told Tiki as she trotted beside me, keeping a watchful eye on the box I carried. "But I don't mind a bit. Finding you and your babies is the best Christmas gift I could imagine."

We turned into the cul-de-sac that held the former model house that Auntie and I now occupied. Aunt Fae and Keone, conversing in the driveway, turned in my direction.

Their faces mirrored astonishment, then joy, as they spotted Tiki beside me. "Oh, thank goodness!" Aunt Fae exclaimed, covering her heart with both hands. "Tiki is finally home!"

"And what've you got in that box?" Keone asked, quirking a brow. "You're carrying it like it's something special."

"The most special ever," I said. "Let's go inside before I show you."

I wanted to get the kittens safely indoors in case Tiki acted up in the presence of others; but my former hellcat remained calm, trotting close beside me as I reached the front door and opened it by depressing the handle with my elbow.

"Glad I've got long pants on this morning," Keone joked as he followed me. Tiki had taken a swipe at his legs on more than one occasion.

"Especially when you see what I've got in the box," I said. "Stay at a distance. Let's see how our girl adjusts to being inside."

Keone's eyebrows went up and so did Auntie's, but neither argued as I led the way with Tiki close beside me. I slowly lowered the container to the floor in front of the decorated driftwood tree.

Tiki hopped into the box as soon as it hit the floor. The kittens mewed and scrambled, milling around their mother. Keone and Auntie, eyes wide, took in the sight.

Auntie's knees seemed to give out and she collapsed on the ottoman. "Oh, my heart!"

"Tiki's been busy!" Keone's chuckle filled the air. He approached and reached forward, very slowly, as if to touch a kitten.

Tiki flattened her remaining ear and narrowed her eyes.

He withdrew his hand. "Okay, mama. No means no."

Auntie cupped her cheeks with her hands, gazing into the mass of milling kittens with Tiki seated upright among them, beaming with pride. "This is so . . . omigosh. I have no words."

"I know," I said. We smiled at each other. "Just the best Christmas ever."

"And the day has just begun," Keone said, slinging an arm around each of us. "So glad to be a part of it with two of my favorite ladies—and Tiki and her family, too."

"And a very merry Christmas was had by all," Auntie said, and dashed the moisture off her cheeks with a smile.

EPILOGUE

THE WEEKS FOLLOWING that enchanted Christmas Day whizzed by faster than a surfer shooting the tube on a giant wave at Banzai Pipeline. Life in our little corner of Maui was much like the island itself - vibrant, full of life, and now, teeming with kittens.

Tiki's little ones grew fast, their antics evolving from clumsy explorations to deliberate, albeit pint-sized, adventures—such as tipping over the driftwood tree and pulling off all the ornaments while Auntie and I were away. The once serene ambiance of our home was gone like a beach at high tide, replaced with a whirlwind of kitten exploits.

Aunt Fae and I dwelt in what I referred to as a 'kitten tsunami.' The fallen petals of hibiscus and bird of paradise flowers from knocked over vases were strewn about like confetti after a festival. The curtains looked like they'd had an unfortunate encounter with a mini lawn mower, and the toilet paper rolls had to be put up above the tanks to avoid being unrolled daily like crepe paper at a party.

The chaos was fun, but a bit much—at any given time we'd arrive home to find five kittens climbing on every available surface and one aggrieved-looking Tiki trying to ignore their frequent roughhousing ambushes.

As soon as the babies were eating solid food, we decided to pass on their unique joy and shenanigans to a few special people. With Tiki's blessing (she was as fed up as we were), Auntie and I packed all of the kittens into the carrier and took Tom and Jerry to their new home with Opal and Artie.

After that happy stop (they'd been excitedly waiting and had all the supplies on hand a pair of rowdy twin boys would need), we drove the golf cart with the remaining three kittens in the carrier up to the Nakasone home on Plumeria Street.

The afternoon sun slanted over poufy cumulous clouds, and a gentle tropical breeze carried the scent of plumeria and pikake from neighboring yards as we rolled up the street. The faint strains of a distant ukulele added a backbeat to the noise of three kittens mewing in the carrier.

The girls' father Joe and I had already talked, and we'd decided to keep the kittens' arrival a surprise—though Joe and the girls' aunt Lani had been secretly collecting beds, flea collars, toys, and a covered litter box to prepare for the big day.

We turned up the Nakasone driveway at last, taking in changes since our last visit. "Nice to see the yard mowed," Auntie commented in an aside. "The place is looking better."

"Joe told me his construction company opened a satellite office in Hana. So he's working a lot closer to home now," I said. "Looks like he has a little more time with his girls."

Joe must have heard us coming, because he opened the front door and stepped onto the porch. A reserved man with circles of fatigue under his eyes all the times I'd seen him at the post office, today his hair was neatly cut and damp from a shower; his shirt and pants were fresh.

"Aloha, Kat and Auntie," Joe said with a smile I'd never seen before. "I can hardly wait to tell the girls. You're going to make their year with this."

"And you'll be doing us a favor, giving two of these rascals a good home," I said, putting the brake on the golf cart.

"I told the girls to wait in the back room, that I had a surprise coming." Joe's dark eyes sparkled. "It's been so long since we've had any fun around here."

"Well, that's all about to change," Aunt Fae said, opening the carrier and taking out a kitten. She handed it to him. "Here you go. They can choose two out of three, and we'll keep the one that's left."

Joe held the little creature—the runt of the litter, the tiny calico —against his broad chest. His work worn hands stroked the soft fur gently. When he looked up, tears glistened in his eyes. "Thank you, ladies. For all you've done to make the holiday special for the girls, and for making sure they didn't get in trouble for stealing Lady Sapphire. And for these." He gestured to the kittens.

"You're welcome," I said briskly. "What are neighbors for? Now let's get them inside and surprise the heck out of your daughters."

Holding the purring bundles of energy, the three of us entered the threadbare but neat living room. I remembered the couch well from when Lady Sapphire gave birth to her kittens there.

Aunt Fae tossed a fleece blanket we'd brought onto the carpet, and we set the three kits down on it.

"Get in here, girls!" Joe bellowed, making Aunt Fae and I jump with his volume—but he was grinning as he yelled.

"Coming, Dad!" Sandy and Windy hurried out of their bedroom and then stopped in their tracks, tripping over each other, at the sight of the kittens.

"Did you bring us . . . kittens?" Sandy asked, meeting my eyes, her voice a mixture of hope and disbelief. Windy clung to her sister, her eyes huge and fixed on the blanket and its contents.

The three curious babies were already creeping in different directions on the blanket, whiskers aquiver, eager to explore their new environment.

"We certainly did," I confirmed. "Meet three mischief makers from the mighty line of Tiki. Your dad said you can each choose one to keep."

As if understanding their introduction, the kittens decided it was showtime. They darted around the room, tiny tails waving in the air like palms in a gust of wind. The girls erupted into giggles and fell to their knees to play with the kittens. All three beasties charged them, batting at them with tiny paws and bouncing around on stiff little legs.

"No fear," Joe said approvingly, and then emitted a boom of laughter as the white kitten with the black tail pounced on his sock-clad foot, wrestling it like a lion taking on a hippo.

We eventually left behind the little calico, already called Patches, and the white kitten with the black tail, dubbed Yin-Yang for its opposite colors.

After we bid the Nakasone family goodbye, the backdrop of chuckles and kitten noises following us as we backed down the driveway was the best farewell song.

"I have a feeling things are really going to change around that house, "Aunt Fae said, her voice filled with amusement. "Let's hope their curtains can withstand the onslaught better than ours have. If not, they're in for a 'ripping' good time!"

"And we still have Misty, here, to keep Tiki on her toes. I'm glad we didn't have to say goodbye to all of them," I said. I smiled at the sweet little gray with white socks resting in Auntie's arms as I turned the golf cart toward home. "No need to replace the curtains until she's much older and has settled down a bit."

"Slowly but surely, that model house is becoming our home," Auntie said with satisfaction.

"I couldn't agree more," I said. "We've got a lot to be grateful for."

Though the month had been stressful, in the end I wouldn't change a thing. Aunt Fae and I would always remember our first holiday in Ohia—and if we didn't, Tiki and Misty would be there to remind us.

Keep an eye out for PAU HANA, #5, in 2024!

ACKNOWLEDGMENTS

Aloha dear readers!

Thanks so much for following along with Tiki, Kat and their holiday story. I had such a fun time including ALL THE THINGS I love about holidays in Hawaii! I'm a big sentimental goof about Christmas and love every silly flashing light, tasty treat, and tinkly song about it.

That said, this IS a Toby Neal story—which means I'm tackling a real Hawaii issue, even in an entertaining, feel-good story (as I do in all my books.)

The problem of feral cats in Hawaii is a serious one. Their population impact on the rare, endangered, and endemic species of birds and monk seals in the islands is real. The expense of spaying and neutering is too much for many island folks to bear, and without any natural predators, cats can out-breed humans' attempts to re-home them every time.

What are the answers?

Well, as I've explored in this story, humans have a responsibility to curb the problems they've created through creative and targeted solutions. Cats are some of the most healing and wonderful life companions out there, and no-kill shelters need funding and support. So does the Humane Society which provides most of the low-cost spay/neuter services in Hawaii, as well as abuse protection and animal adoptions.

Sadly, the Hana Bird Refuge is fictional, as is The Cat Shelter, but there are many good private nonprofits doing important work and if you care to, support them with volunteering or a gift anytime!

If you want to stay in the Paradise Crime World longer, we have lots of books for you to explore. You can start this Cozy Mystery series with Kat by reading Coconut Wireless #1, or if you've already done that, check out BLOOD ORCHIDS, Paradise Crime Mysteries #1 with Detective Lei or WIRED ROGUE, second in Investigator Sophie's Paradise Crime Thriller series. Both are FREE at any retailer by hitting the embedded links!

I also invite you to sign up for my newsletter and get a free copy of TORCH GINGER with Lei, set on Kauai! And if you like my voice on the page and are curious about how I came to write these books set in the islands, check out my personal story, FRECKLED: A Memoir of Growing Up Wild in Hawaii. I promise you it's truth stranger and more inspiring than fiction.

And if you enjoyed this story, PLEASE leave a review on my website or on any book retailer. They mean so much and help other readers find my work.

And until next time, I hope you'll be reading . . . and I'll be writing!

Much aloha,

ABOUT THE AUTHOR

Kirkus Reviews calls Neal's writing, "persistently riveting. Masterly."

Readers rave: "We love Toby's fast-paced, character-driven stories set in the paradise world of Hawaii. Nobody can read just one!"

Award-winning, USA Today bestselling social worker turned author Toby Neal grew up on the island of Kauai in Hawaii. Neal is a mental health therapist, a career that has informed the depth and complexity of the characters in her stories.

You can get a FREE award-winning, full-length book by signing up for her email newsletter!

http://tobyneal.net/TNNews